BETTER THAN A
Crown

VALERIE COMER

ACKNOWLEDGMENTS

I'm so grateful for each one of my readers and fans! I'm kind of sad that our visits to Helena, Montana, are over. I've been living in this story world since the summer of 2013 and enjoyed every minute spent with all the characters I've come to know and love: Marisa and Jase from *More Than a Tiara*, Bren and Rob from *Other Than a Halo*, and now Heather and Levi from *Better Than a Crown*. I also loved tying this series (most specifically *Other than a Halo*) in with my Urban Farm Fresh Romance series, which features many of Rob Santoro's relatives.

I'm thankful for my friend Angela Breidenbach, Mrs. Montana 2009 and co-author with me of *Snowflake Tiara* (2014), who coached me in the ways of pageantry. She was totally instrumental while I wrote *More Than a Tiara*. Even though she had much less input into the other two novels, I'll always treasure her friendship, the emails, the long Skype calls, and the visit we made to Helena together.

I also appreciate fellow author and friend Elizabeth Maddrey for being a sounding board and encourager so many times during the writing of this story. She also offered valuable input as a beta reader along with Anna and Joy. Thanks to all three for the quick turnaround as deadlines loomed!

Thanks as always for my editor, Nicole, without whose careful eye there would be many more typos, punctuation errors, and story inconsistencies. She's been with me from the beginning, and I'm so grateful.

Thanks to Jim and to our kids, their spouses, and the precious grandgirls. These people are my reason for writing... in many ways, my reason for living.

I'm so grateful for Jesus, aka the Eternal One, who loves us incredibly. We as believers are even called God's joy and crown (Philippians 4:1). The imagery is also vividly presented in these words Isaiah spoke to Jerusalem:

And you will be called something new, something brand new, a name given by none other than the Eternal One. And you will be the crowning glory of the Eternal's power, a royal crown cradled in His palm and held aloft by your God for all to see. Isaiah 62: 2b-3 (The Voice)

Valerie Comer Bibliography

Urban Farm Fresh Romance

0. Promise of Peppermint (ebook only)
1. Secrets of Sunbeams
2. Butterflies on Breezes
3. Memories of Mist
4. Wishes on Wildflowers
5. Flavors of Forever
6. Raindrops on Radishes
7. Dancing at Daybreak
8. Glimpses of Gossamer
9. Lavished with Lavender
10. Cadence of Cranberries
11. Joys of Juniper
12. Together in Thyme

Pot of Gold Geocaching Romance

1. Topaz Treasure
2. Ruby Radiance
3. Sapphire Sentiments
4. Amethyst Attraction

Miss Snowflake Pageant

1. More Than a Tiara
2. Other Than a Halo
3. Better Than a Crown

Farm Fresh Romance

1. Raspberries and Vinegar
2. Wild Mint Tea
3. Sweetened with Honey
4. Dandelions for Dinner
5. Plum Upside Down
6. Berry on Top

Cavanagh Cowboys Romance
(Montana Ranches Christian Romance)

1. Marry Me for Real, Cowboy'
2. Give Me Another Chance, Cowboy
3. Let Me Off Easy, Cowboy

Saddle Springs Romance
(Montana Ranches Christian Romance)

1. The Cowboy's Christmas Reunion
2. The Cowboy's Mixed-Up Matchmaker
3. The Cowboy's Romantic Dreamer
4. The Cowboy's Convenient Marriage
5. The Cowboy's Belated Discovery
6. The Cowboy's Reluctant Bride

Garden Grown Romance
(Arcadia Valley Romance)

1. Sown in Love (ebook only)
2. Sprouts of Love
3. Rooted in Love
4. Harvest of Love

Riverbend Romance Novellas

1. Secretly Yours
2. Pinky Promise
3. Sweet Serenade
4. Team Bride
5. Merry Kisses

valeriecomer.com/books

A black sports car pulled into Grizzly Gulch Resort's paved parking lot and came to a stop, the purring motor abating into silence.

Heather Francis lifted her cordless drill and tightened the bolt holding the bench on a wooden picnic table. She kept half an eye on the car, waiting for the occupant to emerge. She shouldn't be so nosy, but how could she help herself, knowing her friend's brother-in-law would be arriving today? The man Aimee said was the sweetest guy and best chef in the world... at least next to her husband.

"Uncle Levi!" a young girl squealed. Eight-year-old Shelby scampered across the yellowing lawn as the man climbed out of the low-slung car. He caught the girl, swung her around, then flung her over his shoulder, holding her ankles. Then his gaze landed on Heather.

She gulped and revved the drill, but looking away was beyond her ability at the moment. Aimee was right about one thing. Levi Esteban was sizzling hot. The man wore black from his cowboy hat right down to the pointy toes of his cowboy boots. His snap-front shirt accented broad shoulders that tapered to a narrow waist, where belted black jeans took over. Even his hair, curling out from beneath that hat, was all but black. Whoa.

He raised his eyebrows in Heather's direction, and she waved. Except it was the hand holding the drill, and her finger convulsed against the trigger.

Zing. Zing. Zing.

Heat flooded her face. Could she come off as any more of a moron? And why had she thought catching a glimpse of the man was worth being identified first as a Jill-of-all-trades? But he wasn't supposed to notice her. Not now. Not today. Not like this. She'd only wanted to see for herself before Aimee introduced them like she'd promised.

Still staring, Heather lowered the drill to the table and let go. *Thud.* She yelped as pain shot from the bridge of her foot and tears sprang to her eyes.

Somehow, she'd missed the table. How had that happened? Why did she have to be so klutzy? And in front of Aimee's brother-in-law, no less. There'd be no way he'd look at her twice now, not with anything other than distaste or pity in his eyes.

She turned away, chomping down on her lip, and leaned down to pick up the drill. Ow. Ow. Ow. Her foot hurt like nothing else had since that elbow in her eye years ago. Who knew a ten-pound tool could cause this much pain?

In a minute she'd peek and make sure the man and his niece were out of sight. Then she'd yank off her steel-toed boot, assess the damage, and cry. Definitely cry.

Stupid, stupid Heather.

"Hey, are you okay?" asked a masculine voice. "Looked like that must have hurt."

Heather cringed, not looking up. Couldn't he just go away? Couldn't he have amnesia and forget this ever happened? Couldn't *she* have amnesia?

"You might want to get that boot off before your foot starts to swell."

She'd get right on that if he'd only leave her alone.

"Here, sit down, and I'll give you a hand."

"No. No, I'm okay." *Liar.*

Warm hands caught her shoulders through her hoodie and gently pushed downward.

Heather sank to the picnic bench and allowed her shoulder-length blond hair to curtain her burning face. This seriously couldn't be happening.

Shelby knelt in front of her, peering up. "Miss Heather?" The little girl wore a worried frown.

Please, why couldn't they leave her alone?

"Which one did it land on?" asked the male voice. "Your right?" Long tanned fingers loosened the laces of her boot, nearly hidden behind the cowboy hat as he bent over.

Heather choked back a gasp at the new flood of pain, but a hitch in her breath likely gave her away.

He gave a nervous chuckle. "This might hurt a bit."

You think?

He grasped her boot and, with a deft twist, pulled it off.

Heather tilted on the bench as pain swarmed her senses. No, she couldn't pass out. She needed to stay alert. Get rid of this man. Hobble or crawl to her staff suite in the Tomah House across the resort's grounds.

"Shelby, sit beside her, and let her lean on you."

Like an eight-year-old could prevent her from toppling. Still, the little girl wedged against Heather's side. "It's okay, Miss Heather. Uncle Levi will take care of everything."

He rolled the sock off and tucked it in her boot. Warm hands engulfed her foot, thumbs gently probing the bridge of it. "I don't think it's broken, but you should probably have an x-ray to be sure." He gave a wry chuckle. "Good thing those are steel-toed boots."

Too bad it hadn't been complete medieval foot armor. Heather willed her voice to be steady. "I honestly think it will be okay. It's not the first time I've dropped something." Not usually as heavy as that drill, though, and not usually on her foot. "I'm sorry for distracting you from whatever you were doing." For calling attention to her clumsiness.

She could just see Mom's disapproving head-shake. *A little more gracefulness, Heather Jeannine. Remember your training.* Right, those twenty-seven pageants had a purpose. To make Mom proud.

"Are you sure? Try putting some weight on it." His hands settled on her waist and lifted.

Heather pushed his hands away. "I don't even know you."

The black cowboy hat tilted up and astonishingly green eyes assessed her from where he knelt in front of her. A grin softened his sober expression and crinkled the skin around those amazing eyes. Aimee had somehow missed mentioning them. "Levi Esteban, at your service. Shelby knows you, so I'm guessing you've met my brother, Jared, and his wife, Aimee?"

She nodded. "I'm Heather Francis. Someone who shouldn't be allowed near power tools." Now, why had she said that? Maintenance was part of her job description at Grizzly Gulch Resort. That, and coaching junior contestants for the Miss Snowflake Pageant... both of which required more dexterity than she'd shown in the last five minutes.

"Now that we've officially met, Heather, can you try standing on that foot?"

Why did the guy have to be so doggone persistent? He wasn't going to take no for an answer.

Heather braced both hands on the bench, sucked in a deep breath, and pushed herself upright. She could do this. She only needed to keep her face emotionless long enough to pass his inspection. Then she'd sit back down until he was out of sight, and *then* she'd crawl to her apartment.

She grimaced as the world wobbled.

"Carry her boot, Shelby."

And that was all the warning Heather had before Levi's strong arms swept her off her feet.

LEVI ESTEBAN STRODE across the leaf-strewn yard toward the front doors of the Grizzly Gulch Resort, carrying Heather. She wasn't all that heavy, even wearing one steel-toed boot. Hot pink nail polish gleamed from the toes of her other foot. He'd nearly burst out laughing when he'd rolled her gray woolen sock out of the way. Who'd have guessed a woman wielding a drill had such a feminine side?

Shelby dashed ahead, triggering the resort's automatic door, and Levi followed his niece inside. He headed across the lobby to the cowhide-covered couches cozying up to the massive rock fireplace, flickering with warm flames.

He didn't really want to set Heather down. She'd closed her eyes, probably to avoid having to look at him while he carried her. Unless she'd fainted from embarrassment? He gave her a little shake. "Heather?"

For just a second eyes the color of the Montana sky blinked up at him from below long dusky lashes in a very pretty face. Her shoulder-length blond hair splayed across the black of his shirt. Then she pushed against him.

Levi lowered her to one of the couches, his arms suddenly cold. Empty. He forced himself not to shake his head. His arms should be used to having no one to hold. He'd sworn off having women in his life, and he'd only be in Helena, Montana, for a month or so. He'd fill in for Jared and be back in Seattle in no time, refreshed and ready to step back into his demanding career. Or, better yet, land the executive chef position at the new location his bosses were opening in a few months. Maybe — eventually — he'd meet someone who could put up with him and his life.

That woman was not in Helena. She was not Heather Francis.

He took a step back just as Aimee followed Shelby into the lobby from double doors open to the dining room.

"Levi! So good to see you." His sister-in-law gave him a quick hug then turned to sit beside Heather. "Shelby told me you hurt your foot. You okay?"

Heather's gaze flashed to Levi's then back to Aimee. "I just dropped a drill on it. I'm fine."

He doubted that but, if she wanted to lie about it, it was her problem.

"I'll get Mrs. Mackie. She's a nurse." Aimee began to rise, but Heather's hand restrained her. The perfectly manicured nails matched her toes.

Levi choked back a smirk.

"No, don't bother her." Heather sucked in her lower lip for a second. "You guys go on and do whatever it is you were doing before I sidetracked you."

Aimee searched Heather's face. "If you're sure."

Heather nodded.

"Here's your boot, Miss Heather." Shelby set it on the floor by Heather's foot.

"Thanks, sweetie."

Aimee looked up at Levi. "Ready to meet Dr. Mackie? He's in his office."

"As ready as I'm going to get." He grinned at her. Jared was lucky to have found this woman. Lucky to have escaped the ghetto of foster care more intact than Levi had, but then, his brother hadn't been in the system as long. Now Jared had everything. A great job as a chef, a beautiful wife, and a lovely daughter — soon to be two when he and Aimee returned from China with the newest little Esteban.

Levi followed Aimee up the split-log staircase. He'd visited Grizzly Gulch Resort once before but never dreamed of working here amidst its rustic splendor. Rounded log walls rose to soaring spaces intersected by pegged log beams, where antler chandeliers dangled from thick chains.

A far cry from the sophisticated ambience of the Fireweed Restaurant. That was okay. He'd finally cashed in his holiday time after three years, and the western décor felt like vacation.

Levi glanced over the log railing from the mezzanine level to the lobby below only to see Heather hobbling toward the door. She should stay off that foot longer. It looked so painful. A bruise would likely appear by tomorrow, and she'd be lucky to wedge her foot into that steel-toed boot anytime in the next week.

Aimee tapped on an office door that stood slightly ajar. "Dr. Mackie?"

"There you are, Aimee. Have you brought Jared's brother?"

She tossed a grin over her shoulder. "I have. Come on in, Levi." She led the way into the room.

Levi blinked. If it weren't for the log wall opposite him, he'd think he stood in a Wall Street office with its minimalist design. His gaze fixed on the man standing behind the sleek glass and steel desk that could have belonged in the Fireweed. "Dr. Mackie? Pleased to meet you. I'm Levi Esteban." He reached for the older man's hand. Firm grip.

"Pleased to meet you, too, Chef Levi. My wife and I are delighted to have you join us at the resort for the next few weeks. The Fireweed's loss, but our gain."

A flush worked its way up Levi's neck. "Thank you. It's good to be here." He wouldn't let the resort owner know how desperately he needed this break. Watching the bosses' nephew learn the ropes was painful.

"Chef Jared and Aimee are leaving for China — what day is it again, dear?"

"A week from Monday," Aimee replied.

"Right. In nine days. I'd like you to work every shift with Jared before then, so you can learn how we do things here at the Gulch. Then you're on your own for a month or so, running the kitchen daytime from Tuesday through Saturday." The dark gray eyes assessed Levi from below thick gray hair streaked with faded red. "Are you up for that?"

"Absolutely." Levi gave a firm nod. It would be a stroll on the beach after dinner rush in Seattle.

"On Friday, there's overtime during our annual Halloween party for the residents of Helena, which the kitchen staff has already begun prepping for." Dr. Mackie turned to the window, pulled back the vertical blinds, and pointed out. "The event takes place there in the open area by the pavilion. We set up tents for the food and some games, have a bonfire, a costume contest for the children..." He leaned closer to the window, and a frown appeared as he gazed down. "What on earth?"

"Excuse me, sir?" asked Aimee.

"It's Heather Francis. She's..." He shook his head. "She appears to be crawling across the lawn."

CHAPTER 2

*C*rutches.

Heather loathed the things, but a gal had to get around somehow. Her face still burned at the memory of Levi Esteban scooping her into his arms for the second time and carrying her up two flights of stairs to her apartment in Tomah House. She was not overweight — Mom would never have stood for that — but she weighed more than a bag of feathers.

After depositing her on her own sofa, he'd jogged down to the ice machine on the first floor, fished a towel out of her bathroom, and fashioned an ice pack for her throbbing foot.

Mrs. Mackie had come by later with a set of crutches and a smothering of concern, but the retired nurse didn't think the cuneiform bone was broken. She'd offered Heather stronger painkillers, a fresh ice pack, and a few days off.

That had been two days ago. Now it was Monday noon, and Heather set the crutches beside her chair in the dining hall with her back to the table where Aimee, Jared, and Levi sat with Kristen and Todd, the Mackies' daughter and son-in-law, who helped run the resort. Well, Kristen did. Todd managed an ad agency downtown.

"Hey, Heather." Marisa Mackie dropped into the chair beside her. "I heard you hurt your foot. Not broken, right?"

"Hi, yourself. No, it's only bruised." Not that Heather had gone to urgent care for an x-ray. "It was just me, being clumsy."

Marisa pinned her with a look. "You're not clumsy. I happen to know you're poised and coordinated."

Her friend was describing herself, not Heather. Marisa had been crowned Miss Snowflake two years ago, and Heather had only been third runner-up. Not only had Marisa won the tiara, but Jase Mackie, the pageant photographer, had offered her a stunning diamond just before the announcement in a proposal that had all the contestants dabbing their eyes.

They were so adorable together it made Heather's teeth clench even while she counted Marisa one of her closest friends. Was it too much to ask for a man to sweep her off her feet like Jase had done Marisa? Um... swept off her feet because of love and undying passion, not because she'd dropped a drill on her own foot like some idiot. That definitely didn't count.

"Do you think you'll be up to helping at one of the stations Friday night at the Halloween party?"

"Sure." Heather grimaced. "Well, at least if there's a stool I can sit down on."

"Kristen and I are working out the final details, and I'm

happy to add your name to the volunteer list. I'm sure we can find a sedentary job for you."

"That'd be great. I'll go crazy if I'm totally relegated to the sidelines."

Marisa chuckled and poked Heather's arm. "I'm right there with you, sister. Are you going to need a hand with your pageantry prep classes?"

The after-school classes on etiquette and deportment for the girls considering entering the Snowflake Pageant had begun in late September. "I canceled them for tomorrow. I'm sure I'll be doing better by next week."

"Girl." Marisa stretched out her manicured hand. "It's okay to ask for help."

"But you're so busy, and it's not your job."

"I'm not too busy to help out a friend in need. Okay? Last year when Jase's parents hired you to take over for me, I was still Miss Snowflake and trying to plan a wedding. Life's a whole lot less hectic now."

Heather took in Marisa's face. "Does that mean you want the coaching job back?"

The other woman didn't even hesitate. "Not at all, but I'm happy to help if I'm in Helena, which won't be all the time. Jase and I are headed to Nicaragua to shoot another documentary next week. It looks like we'll be back just before Thanksgiving."

"Oh, I'm glad you'll be home in time. You'd miss having your family around you. Yours and Jase's, both."

Marisa shrugged. "We're on the mission's timetable, not ours. Besides, there's nothing like supporting food efforts in a developing country to make us truly thankful for what we have at home."

"Makes sense."

"You going home for Thanksgiving or staying here?"

"Missoula is close enough I can go for the day. There's too much going on here at the resort that weekend to take the whole four days off, what with the pageant banquet Saturday night and all." One day was about all Heather could handle, anyway. It offered plenty of time for Mom to remind her of all her failings.

"Right. How many girls do you have entering the Little Miss or Junior Miss segments?"

The girls would be introduced at the banquet, even though the pageant proper took place the week before Christmas. "Not all of them have decided for sure, but it looks like six or eight in each level. Plus, we've had others register who aren't in our classes."

"That's terrific! They must be so excited. What a good experience for them."

Obviously, Marisa hadn't endured unending pageants as a child. Heather shrugged. "So long as their parents aren't putting undue pressure on them. In the program, I try to make it all about self-confidence and poise." Ha. She was the wrong person to mentor the girls. One of these days the Mackies would figure out she lacked the very skills she taught, and she'd be out of a job. Would Habitat for Humanity even want her back? Because she wasn't quite ready to put that degree in finance to work.

Marisa's perfectly manicured hand rested on Heather's arm. "Not everyone has a mom like yours, although Priscilla Abercrombie is a valid runner-up. Olivia and Emily are lucky to have you for a coach and mentor."

Heat flooded Heather's face. "Thanks. I try."

"And you're good at it." Marisa's gaze flicked past Heather's head then back. "Hey, have you met Jared's brother yet? He's cute. Single."

"We've met."

Marisa leaned closer, her brown eyes sparkling. "Did I mention cute? And single?"

Heather managed a grin. "You did."

"And a Christian."

"That's great." Heather stretched her leg, her foot throbbing. "Time for me to get back to my place for painkillers."

"Aw, I'm so sorry."

"It's not your fault. All mine. Who drops a drill on her own foot, after all?"

Marisa searched Heather's eyes. "Accidents happen. Don't beat yourself up for it."

Right. Accidents did happen. Why else wear steel-toed boots to start with? But she'd never done something this stupid because she was distracted by a guy.

Who was cute, single, and a Christian.

And knew she was a klutz.

WHY LEVI'S attention was drawn to Heather, he had no clue. Maybe because he felt somewhat responsible for her accident. He'd driven into the parking lot and distracted her... but even that didn't make sense. He wasn't distraction-worthy. He was just a twenty-eight-year-old guy who'd wasted most of those years, one way or another, and was finally on track to make something of himself. Or, more accurately, depending on God to rescue him from the ashes of his life.

Conversation swirled around his table as, across the dining room, Heather got to her feet and tucked the crutches under her arms. The brunette beside her gave her a hug and walked beside her as far as Levi's table.

Heather's eyes caught his and flared as she bit her lip.

It was a crazy thought, but she seemed as aware of him as he was of her. Huh. Something to consider later, in private.

No, it wasn't. He was only here a few weeks then returning home. There wasn't time or room in his life for dating. He fixed the image of the Fireweed's newest location near the waterfront in Seattle firmly in mind. Gisele would name him executive chef before it opened. That was his destiny.

"Join us?" asked Kristen.

Right. There were half a dozen people around the table. No one needed to catch him staring at Heather.

"Don't mind if I do," said the brunette, slipping into the seat between Kristen and Aimee.

Heather shook her head. "I'm late for a date with my painkillers."

Aw, man. "Want me to run get them for you? I'd only be a minute." It was the least he could do. He remembered where the bottle sat the other day by her bathroom sink.

"No. It's okay. Thanks, though." She backed up a step then broke the connection and swung for the doors to the lobby.

"Have you met my sister-in-law?" Kristen's voice drew his attention back.

He smiled at the stunning new arrival. "No, I don't believe so."

"This is Marisa. She's married to my little brother, Jase, who's around here somewhere." Kristen peered around the sparsely populated dining room then shrugged. "Marisa, this is Jared's brother, Levi. He's filling in for Jared while they go to China."

Marisa's smile was model-perfect. "I'm pleased to meet you, Levi. Welcome to Grizzly Gulch Resort. Have you been to Montana before?"

"Nice to meet you, too. I visited when Jared and Aimee first moved here last year. Seems like a nice enough city."

Her eyes lit up. "Oh, Helena is wonderful! Did you know that in the late eighteen hundreds, it was the wealthiest city in the world per capita? They were pulling so much gold out of Last Chance Gulch they barely knew what to do with it all. While you're here, you should have a tour of the Capitol building. The architecture and the murals and stained glass are incredible."

Aimee chuckled. "That's the problem with Jared and me leaving Levi here on his own. With Shelby, I mean. We won't be here to show him around."

"Jase and I will be gone, too." Marisa pulled her face into a moue of disappointment then pointed at Kristen. "That leaves it to you and Todd to make sure Levi sees the city. Oh, don't forget the Cathedral of Saint Helena." Her finger swung to Levi. "You should get a ticket to Christmas in the Cathedral. It's absolutely amazing with the Helena Symphony and—"

"That's the second weekend of December, right?" asked Aimee. "We'll be back by then with our new daughter."

Levi got a word in edgewise. "Which means I won't be here."

Marisa turned back to him. "Oh, you can't leave before Christmas! You need to be around family." Her finger drew a circle around the table. "You probably don't have anyone but Jared, since I know Jared doesn't have anyone but you, so we're all your family."

"I, uh..." That was an overwhelming thought. Levi barely felt like he fit in with his brother at all. Jared was so much older. He was still amazed his brother and sister-in-law trusted him not only with Jared's job, but with their daughter for a month. But how hard could it be caring for an eight-year-old? Especially with the resort owners avowing support.

Aimee nudged Jared. "We should buy our tickets to Christmas at the Cathedral before we leave. I bet they'll be sold out by the time we get back from China."

"Good idea," said Marisa. "I should do the same. And Levi, you really need to consider staying until the new year unless you have major plans elsewhere. There's so much going on, both at the resort and in the city."

Is this where he said he wasn't really the sort to enjoy a bunch of activities? Being a workaholic like he was tended to make a guy a loner. Or was he only a loner because he didn't have a group of friends like the crew around this table? What would it feel like to belong somewhere? Family, friends, a home church?

A wife and children of his own?

Yeah, wasn't going to happen. Not with the hours he'd put in as the Fireweed's executive chef.

CHAPTER 3

"Where do you need me?" Heather leaned on her crutches at the resort gazebo Friday evening. "I can check tickets here if you want." It had been an entire week since she'd dropped the drill, leaving a large purple bruise and a foot too swollen for most of her shoes. Walking like a normal human being was still beyond her reach.

With a smile, Kristen glanced up from where she'd checked the tickets of the most recent guests. "Can you give the chefs a hand in the food pavilion? They're short-staffed."

"I, um. I could. Unless there's someone who needs help more." Someone clear across the lantern-lit clearing, far away from Levi Esteban's shockingly green eyes.

"That's our biggest need tonight. Axel phoned in sick."

Heather took a deep breath. "Okay. If you're sure."

Kristen angled her head and narrowed her eyes. "Pretty sure, yes. Is that a problem for some reason?"

"No. No problem at all." Heather clutched at one faint hope. "So long as there's a place to sit down."

"Aimee made sure of that. And before you ask, she's tied up with the kids' games, which you cannot do with a bunged-up foot." Kristen's eyebrows rose into her luscious red-gold hair. "If I didn't know better, I'd think you didn't want to be around food. Or possibly our new chef."

"Oh, no. Everything's fine." Heather scanned the area and found the well-lit pavilion where the white-coated brothers worked together. She swallowed hard. Short of telling Kristen she wouldn't do it, she was kind of stuck. "I'll just head over there right now, then. Unless..."

"Levi *is* kind of cute, isn't he?"

Heather's gaze jerked back to Kristen's twinkling eyes. "Lots of guys are cute."

"True." Kristen giggled and turned to the family who'd just approached her table. "Welcome to Grizzly Gulch Resort!"

Heather made her way around the bonfire crackling in the middle of the space, surrounded by a dozen or two chatting people. Assorted games for the kids had been set up on the far side. Aimee would be over there, but that had to be better than extra time with Levi. With her luck, Heather would dump boiling coffee down the front of herself or, even worse, him.

She paused where Bren Santoro tied an apple to a string dangling from a line between two trees. A gaggle of little girls gathered around her, chattering a mile a minute as they took turns handing her apples.

"Hey, Bren. Do you need a hand?" The other woman was

largely pregnant. She shouldn't have to do any bending or lifting.

"Hey, girl!" Bren's face wreathed in a smile. "Good to see you. How are you managing?"

Heather patted her crutches. "Okay, I guess. My foot will take a while to heal."

"That must be so painful. And annoying."

"Definitely annoying."

Lila, Bren's daughter, clunked heads with Shelby Esteban as they both reached for apples in the bucket at the same time.

Bren chuckled. "I think I have more help than I can handle already, but if you're in need of a job, check with Kristen. I'm sure she can put you to work."

Hopefully the semi-darkness would hide Heather's flushed cheeks. "Been there, got the assignment. I just wasn't sure if you might need me more." Oh, that sounded so lame.

"No, the girls are all over it. In fact, I wouldn't mind if Kristen found some of them another assignment. It doesn't take four eight-year-olds to hand apples to a fat woman."

"You're not fat! When is the baby due?"

Bren sighed. "Mid-January, but it can't come soon enough for me. Lila is super excited about the pageant and Christmas, but I can't wait until all that's over and the baby arrives. I hate waddling."

"I hate hobbling, but I imagine I'll be walking normally long before you will."

"No doubt. Where did Kristen assign you?"

"Food." Heather glanced the rest of the way around the perimeter. "I guess I should get over there."

"New chef is quite a looker, isn't he?" Bren chuckled. "Doesn't hold a candle to my Rob, of course, but for a mere mortal, he's pretty hot. And those eyes."

What was this, make-Heather-admit-she-liked-Levi night? She shrugged and turned so the girls couldn't overhear. "Looks aren't everything."

"That's very true, but he seems to be a good guy behind his handsome face. How many men his age would drop everything to help his brother out for a few weeks? Not only on the job, but taking care of a child. You've got to admit, that's not your average man."

Beyond her, Bren's helpers turned toward them, giggling.

Great. That was all Heather needed. "I should be going." She turned her crutches toward the makeshift kitchen.

"Have fun!" called Bren.

She'd try, but Bren's words poked and niggled. It wasn't so much that Levi had been willing to leave his own life behind for a month, but how had it been possible? How many vacation days did he have coming to him from his job? And when Marisa had informed him he should stay until the new year, he hadn't said anything about a job to get back to. What was the scoop on mysterious Levi Esteban?

JARED WAS some kind of crazy over-achiever. He'd taken the Oktoberfest theme and run with it, though Dr. Mackie had offered a firm "no" to the concept of German beer on tap. It was a family friendly event, after all. Now Jared cooked two kinds of sausages plus hot dogs on the gas grill, leaving Levi and Heather with the remaining food.

Not that Levi was watching Heather. He was too busy rolling out, boiling, and baking pretzels in the wood-fired oven that formed the back wall of the outdoor kitchen, but he couldn't help overhearing her chatting with the guests as they came through the line.

He might've snuck a few peeks her way. She looked pretty cute in Axel's white chef coat. It might be much too large for her small frame, but she needed something to cover her gray hoodie. She wore her shoulder-length hair in a French braid — something Aimee had fruitlessly spent the week trying to teach Levi to do on Shelby's hair — and her hands flew as she helped guests load their plates with everything from gherkins to stew to hot potato salad.

A whining female voice came to his attention. "Where are the vegetarian main dishes?"

Levi paused, ready to drop another pretzel in the boiling baking soda bath, but didn't turn around. In his peripheral vision, he saw Heather lean over the serving counter.

"Good evening, Priscilla. The only meat we have are the sausages and hot dogs. Everything else should be suitable for you."

"You expect me to fill up on potato salad and sauerkraut?"

Levi glanced over. The fortyish woman was so thin three bites would fill her to the top.

"It's all very delicious." Heather smiled. "An authentic German selection. What would you like to try? How about you, Emily? Olivia?"

Emily and Olivia? Weren't those the names of the girls

that gave Shelby a hard time for her Latina features? Levi fished the pretzels out of the boiling bath, his ears straining to hear.

"I want a hot dog, Mom," said one small voice.

"Definitely not." The woman's voice dripped with annoyance. "That is the very worst kind of meat. Made of all types of animal byproducts."

Levi bit his lip to keep from laughing out loud. Did the woman know that the German word for sausage, wurst, sounded just like worst?

"Oh, no. These hot dogs are all food-grade beef. There's nothing weird in them. The list of ingredients is on the board over there."

How could Heather remain so calm and cheerful? Levi fished the last of this batch of pretzels from the boiling water and turned to arrange them on the baking sheet.

"It doesn't matter, does it? I'm vegetarian. I would have thought in this day and age, you'd offer a broader selection. I paid enough for our tickets to this event."

He'd had enough. Levi shifted beside Heather and looked the other woman in the eye. "I'm sorry, ma'am. All the advertising clearly announced what type of cuisine to expect this evening. If you'd like a refund, I'm sure Mrs. O'Brien at the reception desk would be happy to give you one, and you can pick up dinner elsewhere."

The woman pulled back her shoulders and gave him a narrowed look. "And who might you be?"

"Chef Levi Esteban." No way was he leaving the title off his name. "An employee of the Grizzly Gulch Resort who's worked a double shift today to provide this terrific German cuisine for our guests." He pointed at the colorful side dishes. "Why not give our red cabbage slaw a try? Or perhaps the kale salad? The next batch of authentic pretzels will be out of the oven in three minutes, if you prefer them hot."

The younger girl tugged at her mother's hand. "Those smell good, Mommy."

Levi slid one onto a plate and held it across the counter. "Here you go."

With one final glare, the girls' mother accepted the offering and added a small dollop of slaw beside it. The two children asked for several of the side dishes, and Heather served them with a smile.

It wasn't until the trio moved away from the serving counter that she slumped back against her tall stool. "That woman," she muttered.

"Who is she?" Levi glanced at the timer and reached for his oven mitts.

"Priscilla Abercrombie." Heather sighed. "Both her girls are in my etiquette classes, but she doesn't miss a beat in every effort to cut me down. I'm pretty sure she wasn't vegetarian last week. I think it was her excuse to be difficult tonight."

Jared stepped closer. "You're probably right. She's unimpressed with the Mackies having hired a Mexican chef." He elbowed Levi lightly. "Now there's two of us. And she doesn't want her girls playing with Shelby."

Levi rolled his eyes. "I can do great things with a vegetarian menu when it's called for, but making a scene when this was clearly advertised otherwise was ridiculous."

"Priscilla says a lot of things that are uncalled for. She's unbelievably proud that Emily was crowned Little Miss

Snowflake last year, and she's decided both girls will win their levels this year."

The pageant. Levi gritted his teeth.

Jared raised his eyebrows. "Isn't that up to the judges to decide?"

"You'd think."

Levi turned to remove the pretzels from the oven then slid in the next trays. This resort was a great place, and he could see why Jared and Aimee were happy here... except for the Miss Snowflake pageant. What was it with women that made them compete with each other for judges to decide who was more beautiful? Not only was it dumb, but anyone could see the judges were biased. Uh, not that he was an expert.

He heard Jared's voice behind him. "Did Aimee get Shelby signed up yet?"

"She did! She's so excited."

Wait a minute. His brother was buying into this thing for his daughter?

Jared chuckled. "Shelby's been practicing her cartwheels all over the house. She says that's her best talent."

"She's shown me." Heather's voice held a hint of laughter. "She's pretty good."

Levi turned back and narrowed his gaze at his brother. "You can't be serious about this. You're telling your daughter that her goal in life is to be pretty?"

"What?" Jared shook his head. "That's not what the pageant is all about."

"Oh? Tell me." Because... yes, it was. He'd followed them for a while, a long time ago.

Jared brandished his tongs toward a group entering the

pavilion. "Later, bro. Or, better yet, get Heather to explain it to you. She's the coordinator, after all."

What? Levi glared at her. "I thought etiquette classes were just that."

"They are." Her chin came up. "We teach manners. We teach poise and confidence. Public speaking."

"And then parade them across a stage wearing swimsuits. Kids their age?" How did women accept being objectified like that? And then there was the Brazilian pageant for which woman had the sexiest bottom. Seriously.

"Miss Snowflake doesn't have a swimsuit competition. At any age level." Heather's words bit off with precision as she leaned over, eyes glittering. "The women's level has a skiwear competition, but if you're worried parkas and snow pants might be too revealing, you'll be glad to know the Little Miss and Junior Miss levels don't even have that."

"They—"

"The girls wear matching navy T-shirts and leggings for everything but the formal wear, and that's just a fancy name for a party dress. There is nothing immodest or wrong about Miss Snowflake."

Whoa. Levi held up both hands, but she kept going.

"Beauty is only skin deep, but poise and personality will give the girls confidence for their entire lives. Any questions?"

Before Levi could form a single thought, a round of applause broke out from the group who'd entered the pavilion. "Go, Heather!"

Great. Not only had he offended both Jared and Heather, but he looked like an idiot in public. He dropped a pretzel into the boiling bath, then another, before shooting a glance at Heather.

Cheeks flushed, she served the newcomers with a gracious smile.

Poise and confidence. She had those in spades.

CHAPTER 4

*C*ould she get out of going to Aimee and Jared's going-away party? Heather growled in frustration as she stared into her closet Sunday after church. She'd built up some hopes — how stupid of her — from all Aimee had said about Levi. How cute he was. How sweet. How single.

All true, but if he had a prejudice against pageantry, he was obviously the wrong guy for a woman who was a veteran of twenty-seven of them. It wouldn't be any consolation that she hadn't won a single one.

No, she needed to attend the event. Aimee was not only her friend, but she and Jared were both fellow employees of Grizzly Gulch Resort. Heather couldn't skip the staff party celebrating the Estebans' trip to China to pick up little Mei from the orphanage. She'd just avoid Levi. Shouldn't be hard in a group of over two dozen, since she hadn't been assigned to help him serve refreshments this time.

She tugged her best new jeans up then slid a royal blue top over her torso, smoothing the lace overlay as she angled herself at the full-length mirror. Yep, the color drew out the blue in her eyes. Not that they'd ever pop as much as Levi's green orbs. Such a striking, unusual color. Where did they come from, anyway?

Never mind. She pulled her hair toward the top of her head. Up or down? Hmmm. A casual bun today. All this paying attention to her looks had nothing to do with Levi Esteban. Nothing at all. He had no use for girly girls, and — her years of working for Habitat for Humanity aside — she was one through and through.

His loss.

Levi thought pageants were dumb, but what did it matter? He was only here for a few short weeks. He'd be long gone before the festivities started. Heather would forget all about him in no time at all, and one day she'd meet a terrific man who understood her and loved her. Unless she'd stay a runner-up forever.

If only she could wear heels, but the swelling hadn't receded enough for that. The slipper on her foot and the crutches under her arms would be her constant companions for at least a few more days.

She swung across the leaf-strewn lawn to the lodge. Brrr. Now that November had arrived, the outside air held a definite hint of frost. The automatic doors slid apart at her approach, welcoming her into the warmth of the lobby where a fire crackled in the massive fireplace.

Heather followed the voices and laughter toward the open dining room doors. A quick glance around revealed Levi laughing with his brother and Rob Santoro over near the food. Good thing she wasn't hungry, right?

"Miss Heather!" Shelby bounced to her elbow, Lila Santoro and Charlotte O'Brien in tow.

"How's your foot, Miss Heather?" asked Charlotte, her winsome red-gold curls tied back with a green ribbon.

"Doing better every day." Most days that seemed true. "I'll be walking again in no time."

"How can you teach us to be ladies if you can't walk?" Lila batted her eyelashes.

Heather chuckled. "Ladies do more than walk, you know." She turned to Shelby. "I hear you are going to be in the pageant." Hopefully that wasn't supposed to be a secret.

Shelby brightened. "I am! Mommy said it would give me something to think about while she and Daddy are away. I'm going to be a lady who does cartwheels." She turned to her friends. "What are you going to do?"

"I sang a song last year," said Lila. "Maybe I will again."

"And I played piano," put in Charlotte. "I'm much better at it now. It was a baby piece then."

"You both did a great job, and I'm sure you'll do well this time, too. You and your moms don't need to decide about your talent until just before Thanksgiving. We'll need to know in time to put it in the program."

"My mom won't be here then." Shelby's face pulled into a frown. "Maybe Uncle Levi will help me practice."

As if.

Mrs. Mackie bustled over. "Heather, I have a question for you. Sorry to be talking business on a Sunday afternoon."

"Um, no problem. What do you need to know?"

"You know William and I are trying to do everything we

can to help Jared and Aimee manage this trip to China to bring home this little girl's sister." She wrapped her arm over Shelby's shoulders and squeezed.

"Yes?"

"Well, we overlooked something. William and I hired Levi to replace Jared, forgetting Aimee is usually home with Shelby after school and on Saturdays, and we'd said we'd smooth over everything for their adoption."

Uh oh.

"So I had this crazy idea. You are free to say no, of course."

Not likely, with three curious children taking in every word.

"I know you feel badly being unable to do much of your regular job with that sore foot, so I thought you might be willing to spend some time with Shelby. She's enrolled in the pageantry classes, so she'll be all yours on Tuesday afternoons anyway..." Mrs. Mackie's voice trailed off as her eyes searched Heather's. "We'd pay you your regular wages. It's all to keep the resort running smoothly, after all."

That would mean seeing Levi every day when he got off work. That would mean seeing him Saturdays.

"You'd still keep all your duties for the pageant, but child care would replace your maintenance tasks, just until Thanksgiving. You've already turned off the water and power to the RV park and the cottages, right?"

Heather nodded. "A couple of weeks ago." Guests through the winter roomed inside the lodge, and they'd be full up over Christmas with the pageant and all the winter fun. The housekeeping staff's problem, not hers.

Mrs. Mackie beamed. "Then there's nothing critical in the maintenance department for now. You won't need to push the healing on your foot, and you won't need to worry about your paycheck."

Saying no wasn't an option. Besides, she enjoyed Shelby. Heather could keep time with Levi to a minimum. Or...sShe could pour on her charm and see if three weeks was long enough for him to see her as a desirable woman instead of a bungling Jill-of-all-trades.

Heather straightened as best she could on the crutches. "If it will help the resort run more smoothly, I'll do what I can."

"Yay!" exploded Shelby, flipping into a cartwheel. "I love being with Miss Heather!"

Well, that was nice, right? Until Heather's eyes collided with Levi's narrowed gaze across the room, and the fizzle seeped out of her. Even three *years* wouldn't be long enough.

JARED SMACKED Levi on the back. "Looks like Mrs. Mackie took care of that. I can't believe Aimee and I were so focused on Mei that we didn't think about the gap in Shelby's schedule. Everything's come together so quickly for the adoption."

Levi pulled his eyes away from the gorgeous woman across the dining room. Now he'd be seeing Heather all the time? No way.

Rob Santoro shook his head. "You know we would've been happy to help out, but Bren is exhausted all the time with this pregnancy. Thankfully the CSA arranged volunteers to help put the gardens and greenhouse into winter mode, because Bren sure isn't up to it, and I don't know what to do, being a new farmer and all."

"I don't know how we'd run the resort kitchen without the CSA, man." Jared turned to Levi with a smirk. "At least this time of year you know what will be in those boxes they drop off twice a week. Lots and lots of squash."

"Hey, there's other produce!" Rob protested. "Onions, garlic, brassicas..." He trailed off when Levi and Jared began to chuckle. "Okay, never mind. I don't need to tell you what the market gardeners can do around here."

While the Tomah Community Supported Agriculture program varied some from the box programs Levi had been familiar with in Seattle, he and Jared had gone through the listing and created a loose breakfast and lunch menu for the next few weeks. He'd put his own touch on each recipe, of course. If he could add anything to his repertoire for the Fireweed, he'd do it. A glowing recommendation from Dr. Mackie and his wife would not go amiss in his quest to head up the restaurant's new location.

Shelby darted through the gathering, her two best friends at her heels, then collided with Jared. "Daddy! Miss Heather is going to watch me when I'm not in school and Uncle Levi has to work. We're going to have so much fun. Maybe she'll paint my nails and put cucumbers on my eyes."

Levi stiffened.

Jared chuckled and hoisted his daughter into his arms. "Cucumbers, huh? I thought they were your favorite veggie?" He nuzzled her nose with his own. "To eat."

The little girls giggled and Rob crouched to gather his stepdaughter, Lila, close. "Hey, Princess."

"Hi, Daddy."

Rob couldn't be that much older than Levi, yet the other man had married a single mom and gained two kids. It was obvious Rob adored Lila and Davy as much as he adored their mother. The man's contented gaze constantly sought Bren out across the room.

There was time for a family in a few years. Levi wasn't in any hurry. *Right, God? We've got plans.*

If God wasn't on board with Levi's agenda, He'd need to wallop him good to get his attention. God was big enough to do that, for sure. The memory of the drill falling on Heather's foot brought a lift to his lips. Had that been God's way of getting *her* attention? And, if so, for what?

"Heather!" called Jared.

She maneuvered her crutches and came nearer. "Did Shelby tell you Mrs. Mackie asked me to watch her around your brother's schedule?" She darted a glance at Levi but didn't meet his gaze.

Not that he wanted her to.

"Yeah, she did. That's great. Aimee called around to a few of our friends but no one could fill in as much as we needed, so Mrs. Mackie said she'd make sure everything was covered. I can't thank you enough."

"I'm sure we'll have a good time." She wrinkled her nose at Shelby, who grinned back.

Heather had a great smile and seemed genuinely nice. No wonder his niece liked her. Levi should be glad Shelby would be well taken care of while he worked. Cooking was a rough career for a family man. He supposed his brother was happy to work the day shift when his daughter was in school, even if it didn't leave as much scope for creativity as dinners.

"Sounds like you and Levi will need to coordinate schedules," he heard Jared say.

He blinked back to attention. Everyone was looking at him. "Uh, yeah. We should do that." He dug his phone from his pocket and held it up. "I should... get your number."

Heather's blue eyes collided with his, and that addicting smile crossed her face. "We should." She hopped on her good foot as she tucked both crutches under one arm and tugged her own phone out of her back pocket with her free hand.

If she toppled, he'd have to catch her. But... she wouldn't, would she? Although she'd felt pretty good in his arms the two times he'd carried her.

Another hop and she regained her balance, her face flushing as she rearranged her crutches. She focused on the glittery pink device as her thumbs flew. Then she lifted it to her face and clicked.

She'd taken his picture? Just like that, without asking permission?

Heather glanced up at him. "I'm ready for your number."

Levi gave his head a quick shake and rattled it off as Jared leaned over Heather's shoulder.

"Nice shot of my bro." Jared smirked at Levi.

"Oh." Heather's cheeks reddened. "I'm sorry. I always attach a photo to each contact. I didn't think to ask."

"Great idea." Jared's grin widened. "Levi, you should do

the same, especially here where you don't know everyone yet. It will help you keep people straight."

Could his brother's setup be any more obvious? With Levi's luck, not having a sitter lined up for his daughter was no oversight but a calculated plan to force him into Heather's presence.

Later. Levi would kill his brother later. After he took Heather's photo and recorded her contact information.

CHAPTER 5

*T*he week had gone pretty well, all things considered. Not that Heather had seen much of Levi. He'd texted every day as he got off work, asking her to send Shelby downstairs to meet him at the car for their short drive to Jared and Aimee's house.

She'd been about to check Week One off her calendar when her phone buzzed with an incoming text from Aimee.

What's your Skype handle? What time will Levi come for Shel? Can we Skype with you then? We have something we need to talk to all of you about.

Curiosity burned as she turned away from Shelby and tapped in her reply. But Aimee didn't answer the main question of what the topic might be. What was so important that Heather needed to be included in the call? Why not call when it wasn't so very early in Beijing?

"What does Mom want to tell us?" Shelby narrowed her gaze. "She better not say we can't have Mei after all. We need to get her out of that orphanage."

Heather shrugged. "She wouldn't tell me, but we'll soon find out."

"My new little sister is sooo cute." Shelby did a handstand. After all, this staff apartment didn't have enough room for full cartwheels.

And here Heather had wondered how the little girl felt about adding a sibling to their family. Not after this week. Sure, Shelby missed her parents, but she talked of little besides her new sister.

Heather heard footsteps on the wooden floors in the corridor outside. Hard for anyone to sneak up on her in the aging Tomah House, the only remaining building from the resort's early days. A sharp knock sounded on her door.

She straightened her top and hobbled to open it. Yeah, her foot still hurt, but she could get around some now. Enough to salvage a bit of pride.

"Hey." Levi looked past her to his niece, a slight frown on his face. "Aimee texted me to come here for a Skype call?"

Heather nodded, not that he was looking at her. "She said it was something she needed to discuss with all of us. I opened the program and added her as a contact. I'll just text her and make sure right now is a good time."

His green eyes flicked off hers. "I will." He pulled out his phone and pecked away.

She could have done it in a fraction the time but, whatever. Aimee was his sister-in-law, so it stood to reason he'd take over. Heather couldn't think of a single scenario in which she was needed for an Esteban family discussion.

The laptop trilled, and Heather hobbled across the space and accepted the call. She waved Levi over, pointing at the sofa with the laptop on a box on the coffee table. "I hope you can both see."

Shelby clung to her hand. "But Mommy wanted to talk to you, too."

Heather squeezed back then disengaged. "There isn't room for three of us, and you guys are more important. Go talk to your mom."

Levi settled on the sofa with Shelby snuggled at his side, then tilted the screen slightly. "Hey, Aimee. Jared. What's going on?"

Heather busied herself across the room, checking Instagram on her phone. She felt like an interloper, but that was crazy. Aimee had set this up.

"Remember we told you all about our first visit with Mei a few days ago?" came Jared's voice.

Shelby nodded. "She's so adorable."

"She is." Aimee paused. "And just as sweet in personality. What the orphanage didn't tell us was that she has a special buddy here that she looks after."

"Yun is about a year older, but prospective parents overlook her because she has a cleft palate," Jared put in. "The two girls love each other very much."

"They're extremely bonded," added Aimee. "It's kind of heartbreaking, really."

A short silence followed, during which Heather's imagination filled in Aimee and Jared looking at each other.

Jared cleared his throat. "What we're wondering is, what would you think of having *two* new sisters?"

Shelby leaned closer. "Do you have a picture of... what did you say her name is?"

"Yun. Yes, we do. Be warned, though. She's not as pretty as Mei."

A few seconds later, the little girl cringed back against the sofa cushions. "She's ugly."

"That's why no one wants her, baby," came Aimee's soft voice. "But doctors in America can fix her mouth so no one could even tell. If we leave her here without Mei, I don't think Yun will ever get another chance. I think it will break her heart."

Heather's own heart twisted. She'd always taken her own beauty for granted, but sometimes wished she didn't have it. Then her mom wouldn't have pushed pageantry on her since the Gerber Baby days. Would her parents have loved her if she had been an ordinary-looking child? How about if she'd been born with a cleft palate? No way her mom could have handled that. Apparently Yun's mother couldn't, either. Poor kid.

"That's really rough," Levi said. "I feel sorry for her, but it's not my decision. It's up to you guys."

"What do you think, Shelby?"

The little girl hid behind Levi's shoulder. "I don't want an ugly sister."

"The doctors can fix it, pumpkin," said Jared.

"Let someone else take her home."

"Then we should leave Mei behind, too," came Aimee's voice. "They're best friends, and Mei takes care of Yun."

"Okay. Find a different girl to bring home. A different sister."

"Honey, we could make a big difference for Yun." Jared's voice. "We can give her a chance for surgery and a normal life. A family with sisters and a lot of love."

Shelby crossed her arms and scowled.

Levi patted Shelby's knee. "I'll find you some pictures and show you what kids look like after that kind of surgery, okay? Then you'll see." He glared over at Heather, his green eyes cold. "Remember, being pretty doesn't matter. Being a nice person on the inside is what's important."

His tone implied Heather assumed the opposite. How dare he? He didn't even know her. She couldn't help being pretty any more than Yun could help having a cleft palate. An accident of chromosome alignment in both cases. Levi had no idea how much she'd wished for plainer looks.

"I suppose," whispered Shelby. "Is Yun a nice person on the inside?"

"Yes," answered Aimee. "She loves Mei very much. She's a bit afraid of Daddy and me because we are taking Mei away, but she's still sweet. You don't want her to be afraid or alone, do you?"

Shelby sucked in her lip and shook her head.

Levi looked at the screen. "So that's what this call was about?"

"Right," said Jared. "But it affects you and Heather, too."

Heather's heart stuttered.

"If we go ahead with this, we'll be in China longer. We've talked to the adoption agency and checked with a travel agent, and we should be home a couple of days before Christmas. So... we need to know if you can stay on at the resort, and if Heather's okay with Shelby for an extra few weeks. I hate to ask it of either of you, but it doesn't make sense for us to come home as scheduled just to return later in the winter for Yun."

For the first time since he'd entered her apartment,

Levi's eyes focused on Heather's. And stayed for a long moment.

She cleared her throat. "I, um, I'm sure I could do that, so long as Dr. Mackie agrees. Shelby is in the pageant anyway, so she'll already be at all the extra events as we get closer."

Shelby bolted upright and stared at the computer. "You won't be here for the pageant?"

"Your part is on Christmas Eve. We wouldn't miss it for anything."

Heather heard the unspoken words. *Unless something comes up.* And when traveling and adopting internationally, all kinds of things could come up. Something already had.

"We'll be there, pumpkin," said Jared. "Levi, can you take a longer leave of absence? I wanted to talk to you about it before I called Dr. Mackie."

LEVI SAGGED against Heather's sofa cushions when she removed the laptop. Now Shelby leaned against her at the tiny kitchen table while they looked up before and after photos of cleft palate surgery.

He'd told Jared he could stay, and it was true. Would it affect his hoped-for promotion? It shouldn't, though Gisele wouldn't be happy. He'd barely touched his vacation days for three years. But every additional day would make it that much more difficult to avoid Heather. Especially with that dratted pageant coming up. Opal, the resort's executive chef, had made no bones about being delighted to leave the pageant meals in Jared's hands. Which were now Levi's.

It wasn't the little girls so much, like his niece. Albeit much greater than he would have liked, her part would be very small. But the entire resort would be overrun with a couple of dozen twenty-something women the entire week before Christmas. Model-thin gorgeous women, most of them blonde or fake-blonde, with nothing in their heads beyond batting their false eyelashes at judges who'd probably been bribed. Like the time in—

No. He wasn't going there. No allowing memories of a decade ago to push back into the forefront of his mind.

All he had to do was cook. He didn't have to meet any of them... except Heather. How many times had she walked off with the winning title, anyway? Weren't they crowned queen or something equally ridiculous? Because if it weren't for her obsession with pageantry — or at least with superficial beauty — he could fall for her. Her charms, though, and her pretty smile... all were practiced behaviors for impressing judges. She wasn't real.

It didn't matter. He wasn't staying any longer than he had to. Helena, Montana, was fine, but it wasn't on Puget Sound. It didn't have the culture Seattle did, no matter what Marisa tried to make him believe.

Wait. Aimee had bought two tickets to Christmas at the Cathedral and left them tucked against the mirror frame in the master bedroom. She and Jared wouldn't be back for the event after all. It was only a matter of time before someone thought of that and got the great idea Levi should invite Heather.

Yeah. So not happening. Maybe he'd take Shelby. Surely his niece was old enough to enjoy whatever passed for a symphony out here in Montana.

The two heads bent over the laptop, Shelby's wavy brown hair pressed against Heather's dusky blond. Heather's left arm encircled Shelby's waist, and Shelby leaned in to whisper something. The two exchanged a look and smile.

Levi shook his head, trying to dislodge the vision. It didn't matter that she got along with his niece. She'd still be part of their life here at Grizzly Gulch when he was long gone, only visiting on his occasional vacations. No telling when he'd have time to take another of those, anyway. The promotion would keep him busier than ever.

What were they looking at, anyway? Shelby wouldn't be smiling at cleft palate photos. He got to his feet, crossed the small space, and rested a hand on his niece's shoulders as he leaned in.

Snap.

An image of the three of them stared back at him from the screen, Heather and Shelby smiling at the webcam, and him scowling over Heather's head.

His niece giggled. "Let's retake!"

He forced on a quick smile. It seemed easier than getting out of the camera's view that quickly. *Snap.* But the guy looking back at him from the computer looked only marginally better than the first take.

"Smile, Uncle Levi!" Shelby shot him a grin before turning back.

For some unknown reason, he gave it another try. *Snap.*

Was this... was this what a family looked like? Sure, Shelby was only his niece, and he and Heather weren't together. But had he ever thought what a family would look like to him?

Not with the upbringing he'd had. He'd landed in foster care when he was barely five and Jared twelve. There'd been no loving home where he came from. Not like Heather likely had. Somehow Jared had made it through relatively unscathed, but when the system had separated the brothers, Levi hadn't fared so well. Not that he was into remembering those years in L.A..

Jared had found his love and acceptance in Aimee and Jesus. He'd been the one to introduce Levi to his Savior.

"I'll email you a copy, Levi, to print out for Shelby." Heather looked up at him. Those blue eyes. A guy could drown. She jumped up, wincing. "Or better yet, you sit in this chair and take a picture of just you and her. We were just goofing around. No one needs a copy of the other one."

He backed up, shaking his head.

"I want this one," Shelby begged. "Send it to Uncle Levi, or you print it out for me."

Heather's gaze met his. "I, uh... It doesn't matter. I'll delete these."

"No, Miss Heather. Please."

He managed to shrug. "Go for it. I don't care."

She bit her lip and glanced down at the laptop. "If you're sure."

"Yeah, no problem." He wouldn't have to admit to anyone that he just might forget to delete the email, would he? To remind him of what a family could look like.

A different family with a different woman.

In Seattle.

Years from now.

CHAPTER 6

*P*astor Grunewald leaned over the pulpit, twinkling eyes assessing the congregation. "For the next few Sundays, we are going to look at what the Bible has to say about crowns. It seems fitting as Helena gears up for the third annual Miss Snowflake Pageant."

Always a princess — never the queen. Heather fidgeted in her seat. Whatever the pastor said didn't change the fact she'd never worn a crown and never would.

The pastor chuckled. "Marisa Mackie assures me our snowflake winners wear a tiara, not a crown, but humor me, anyway. While the words are not completely interchangeable, both refer to someone who wins a prize."

Thanks for the reminder I'm a loser.

"In the epistles, Paul refers to the new believers as his joy and crown. He didn't single out one church over the others. If you believe in Jesus Christ as your Savior and Lord, you are part of Paul's vision. In First Thessalonians chapter two, he says, 'For what is our true hope, our true joy, our victor's crown in all this? It is nothing if it isn't you standing before our Lord Jesus the Anointed at his arrival.' That's in The Voice translation, by the way. What does 'in all this' refer to? Earlier in the chapter he commends the Thessalonian church because they stood firm in their faith even when things got rough."

Images of babies and toddlers with cleft palates came to Heather's mind. These little ones didn't suffer because of their faith, but because of a random fluke of nature. They deserved crowns more than she did.

"In Philippians chapter four, Paul says, 'For this reason, brothers and sisters, my joy and crown whom I dearly love, I cannot wait to see you again.' What does it mean to be someone's joy and crown?"

Marisa and Jase. Bren and Rob. Kristen and Todd. Aimee and Jared. The list of devoted couples she knew went on and on. She'd seen the light in their eyes as they looked at each other. If they weren't each other's joys and crowns, she had no clue what the pastor was talking about.

Maybe she didn't, anyway.

"In Isaiah sixty-two, the prophet yearns for Jerusalem in a similar way that Paul aches for the church. Isaiah says, 'You will be called something new, something brand new, a name given by none other than the Eternal One. And you will be the crowning glory of the Eternal's power, a royal crown cradled in His palm and held aloft by your God for all to see.'"

Pastor Grunewald looked out over the congregation above his glasses. Was it Heather's imagination, or did his gaze linger on hers?

"Isaiah goes on to say, 'People won't talk about you anymore using words like 'forsaken' or 'empty.' Instead, you will be called 'my delight." Let that sink in for a minute. We give ourselves labels. We don't think we're good enough. We don't think we're deserving. We see all the ways we fail. Trust me, the residents of Jerusalem to whom Isaiah was speaking failed. The early church failed. But both were still referred to as a crown of joy. A delight."

Would she ever be loved like that? Guilt niggled. As a child of God, she already was. God called her 'My delight,' not 'forsaken' or 'empty.' Not runner-up, but a crown in God's hand, displayed for all the world to see.

Not a loser.

A winner.

It didn't matter how Mom saw her. Heather took a long breath and released it slowly. It didn't matter how Levi Esteban saw her, either. God was the only One who mattered, and she was His delight. Now if only she could remember that when she felt clumsy and awkward.

God's delight.

LEVI HEAVED a sigh of relief when the pastor prayed a benediction over the congregation before dismissing them. God's delight? Hard to fathom for a kid from foster care.

No wonder his brother wanted to adopt Mei and Yun. Yun would never be anyone's crown if Jared and Aimee didn't bring her home. At the same time, he understood Shelby's discomfort and reluctance.

Was Yun God's crown? How could God let so many babies be born disfigured or be abandoned into orphanages like the one in Beijing?

But it was even more uncomfortable to think of himself as God's delight. He'd been forsaken and empty, just like Isaiah referred to Jerusalem. Like Mei and Yun. Could they all be God's crown?

If Pastor Grunewald — and scripture — were to be believed, he already was. But those thoughts were much too heavy for a Sunday afternoon, one of the few days he had to hang out with his niece. The weather had taken a frigid turn, and, when they were getting ready for church, Shelby complained her winter jacket was too small.

And it was. He'd glanced at the newspaper in the dining hall over breakfast — one of the many perks of working at the resort was not cooking when he was off-shift — and noticed one of the big department stores had a sale on kids' winter wear advertised. A text to Aimee had received a thumbs-up that he take his niece out to replace the parka. That had been followed by a request to pick up a few things for Mei and Yun, complete with a list.

Clothes shopping with a girl Shelby's age? He must be absolutely crazy. He wouldn't know a bargain if he tripped over one, let alone what was in style and what wasn't. Although his niece surely had opinions. The question was, could he trust an eight-year-old's judgment?

Across the church foyer, Heather chatted with Bren and Rob Santoro. She tipped her head back and laughed. Obviously she didn't have the same struggles as he did about self-worth. That sermon was going to poke at his brain for days, and the pastor had threatened an entire series on the topic. Left to his own devices, Levi would go to some other church and leave New Song Fellowship for those who could handle the teaching. But he couldn't rip Shelby away from her familiar surroundings and, besides, he'd needed to hear the words.

Maybe he needed Heather's help with the shopping.

Maybe he could pretend to be confident, just for a few hours. Right? Worth a shot. Before he lost his nerve, he strode across the lobby, swerving around a few kids and old women.

He stopped dead in his tracks. Did he really want to ask Heather in front of Rob and Bren?

But it was too late. Rob looked up and noticed him standing a few feet away. "Levi! Good to see you this morning. What do you think of Pastor Grunewald's message?"

Answering that was about as welcome as divulging the reason he'd crossed the foyer. "Uh, good. Insightful. Challenging." Were those enough words? The right words?

Rob nodded as Heather turned toward Levi, her blue eyes widening. "Hi there."

Man, he should have thought this thing through a bit. "Hi, Heather. Bren." Was it polite to keep asking a pregnant woman how she was doing? Probably not, even though he couldn't think of anything else to say.

Bren peered past him. "Anyone seen Davy?"

Whew. Another topic. "No, but Lila is with Shelby."

She nodded. "I see her. Rob, can we get on home? I need a nap in the worst way." She turned back to Heather. "I'm so sorry to run. Growing this baby is taking every speck of my energy these days."

"No problem." Juggling her crutches, Heather hugged her friend as Rob angled into the crowd, looking for their son. A minute later Bren waddled — Levi hated himself for even thinking the word — toward the girls.

"So, uh, hi." *Smooth, Esteban. Real smooth.*

"Hi." Heather's eyes darted to his then back down.

"Your foot feeling any better?"

"Quite a lot, thanks."

Silence. Awkward silence.

"I was wondering..." Man, could he really do this?

Her gaze met his and held for a second. "Yes?"

He was certifiably crazy. "I need to take Shelby shopping for a new winter jacket. Aimee asked me to get some things for the little girls, too." He stuffed his hands into his jeans pockets and scuffed his cowboy boot along the tile floor. "I was wondering if maybe you'd like to come, too. Give me some guidance. But I forgot about your foot, so I totally understand if you don't feel up to it. Or if you have something else to do this afternoon. I mean, I know it's your day off, and—"

"Sounds fun."

Levi's head shot up and their gazes snapped into alignment. "Really?"

She smiled, and her whole face lit from within. "Female plus shopping equals fun."

"But your foot..."

"I've got the crutches. Besides, I haven't been away from the resort for two weeks. You unlocked my jail cell, so don't try to push me back into it now."

"I... okay. I don't want to back out." Suddenly it was true. They could stay focused on his niece. It would all be good. Heather would give him some reason to avoid her — either on purpose or by accident — and then he'd get her out of his mind and refocus on that potential promotion at the Fireweed. All good.

54

"When do you want to go? We could catch lunch at the resort first, if you like. Axel's cooking today."

And look like a couple in front of all the people they worked with? No. He wasn't ready for anything that public. Why hadn't he waited? Texted her after lunch, maybe? Too late. "Or we could get lunch out and go shopping afterward. My treat." And small payment for her help shopping.

"Um, sure. I'd like that. I caught a ride to church with Mackies, so I should let them know."

So much for word not getting out, but probably someone they knew would spot them anyway. Levi rocked on his cowboy boots, hands still shoved deep in those pockets. "Okay. Know anywhere good to go?"

"I'd say the Parrot, but they're closed Sundays." She scrunched her face in thought. "So is the Firetower. Let me think. Taco del Sol is open today, if you and Shelby like tacos. Or any of the fast food places, depending on what's your fancy."

Levi shook his head. "She'd probably prefer a burger and fries, but that's not my scene. I just can't quite bring myself to go there, if you know what I mean."

She giggled. "I get it. I'm not a big fan myself, but occasionally I'm in a rush and hit the drive-through. I pretty much always regret it, though. Taco del Sol is a few steps up, as far as I'm concerned."

"Thanks for not assuming we like tacos, just because we're Hispanic."

Her eyes widened. "It never even crossed my mind."

He managed a grin. "Well, thanks for that. Let me round up Shelby while you let Mrs. Mackie know you don't need a ride."

HEATHER WATCHED Levi stride across the foyer toward the gaggle of girls. Had Chef Levi Esteban actually noticed her?

Because she'd sure been noticing him. She could barely bite back the shriek of excitement that wanted to erupt. Was this a date? It didn't really count if his niece was along, did it? He could have asked Mrs. Mackie or Kristen to get a coat for Shelby, but he hadn't. He'd asked her.

Inside, her heart did a little dance. She turned and whirled directly into Kristen O'Brien. "Oh! You scared me."

Kristen's eyes glimmered with mirth. "A bit unaware of your surroundings, perhaps?"

Not at all. Not in all directions. "I guess so."

Her friend poked her chin toward Levi and his niece. "So tell me what all that's about."

Word was going to get out anyway, right? "We're going for lunch."

Kristen squealed. "Way to go!"

Heather lowered her voice. "Really, it's mostly because he needs to go shopping for Shelby. With Aimee and Jared in China, some of that has fallen on him. And he's chicken."

"Too funny." Kristen nudged her. "Don't waste your opportunity, girl. Carpe diem."

Heather's eyebrows rose along with the flush flooding her cheeks. "Seize the day?"

"Now you're talking. Go on. Have fun. And go get 'em."

"I need to find your mom and let her know I don't need a ride back to the resort."

"I'll tell her. Charlotte asked me to invite Shelby over

this afternoon, but it can wait. Maybe one day after school this week?"

"Not Tuesday, because that's etiquette class."

Kristen nodded. "Let's see about Wednesday, then. I'll talk to Levi." She leaned a little closer. "I'll see if I can find out just what he thinks of you after today's non-date."

Heather swallowed. "Thanks. I think."

CHAPTER 7

a few hours later, Shelby linked her arm through Heather's, her other hand brushing the front of her new pink-patterned parka as she gave a little skip. "Thanks, Miss Heather."

They'd survived. Although getting off the crutches and putting her feet up sounded like a superb idea.

A harried-looking Levi ambled on the other side of Shelby. The man might have zero sense of style but, dagnabbit, he looked good in anything from a chef tunic to a flannel-lined denim jacket. And those faded jeans? Oh, man. Even the cowboy boots he favored when not in the kitchen added to his appeal.

Levi met her gaze over his niece's head. "So, did we get everything?" His eyes all but begged the ordeal to be over.

Shelby had found a few more items she desperately needed, besides clothes and gifts for Mei and Yun. The girl was beginning to embrace the idea of two little sisters.

Heather hid her smirk. "The list is checked off." Literally. "Except for one thing."

59

Both sets of eyes trained on her, so she held the dramatic pose for a few seconds longer. "I think we need a treat for a finale. Hot chocolate and brownies, maybe?"

Shelby gave a sideways hop. "Oh, yes, please!"

She eyed Levi. "There's a coffee shop a few blocks over that makes the most scrumptious brownies ever." Wait, she was in the presence of a chef. Backpedal time. "I haven't tasted your uncle Levi's brownies, though. He's pretty talented, so he might be able to do better."

"*Might?*" Levi raised his eyebrows at her across Shelby. "I don't do *just brownies*." He air-quoted the words then lowered his voice. "I have secret ingredients. And then I add a dollop of freshly churned vanilla bean ice cream and a drizzle of salted caramel sauce on top."

Oh, man. If only her stomach wouldn't growl aloud at the thought of that decadence. "I'll have to reserve judgment, since I've never had yours." They reached the mall exit, and the doors swished open to a cold November drizzle.

"I hate rain," grumbled Shelby.

"Soon we'll have snow." Winter. Heather's favorite time of year.

Levi laughed as he unlocked the car and popped the trunk for their bags and her crutches. "It's rare we get much snow in Seattle. If we get some before I leave, maybe we can go skiing or tobogganing."

"Hiller Farm hosts a sledding party every year in December." Heather buckled herself into the passenger seat. "Everyone brings sleds and tubes and crazy carpets — whatever they have — and there's a bonfire and hot chocolate and fancy cookies and everything. Were you here for that last year, Shelby?"

The little girl leaned forward in the backseat. "We moved here in March. I've never been sledding. I hope we can go."

Heather looked at Levi as he slid into the driver's seat. She probably shouldn't be making promises. "If your uncle has to work, maybe you can come with me."

"Hiller Farm?" He glanced her way. "Isn't that where Rob and Bren Santoro live? They're having a party when she's about to pop that baby?"

Shelby squealed. "Lila's house? I love Lila's house."

Heather chuckled. "It's a bit of a tradition. I'm pretty sure Marisa and her mom and everyone else from the CSA will pitch in. Bren won't have to do a thing."

"Oh, right, they're part of the Tomah CSA." Levi started the car. "We get a lot of vegetables from them for the resort kitchen."

"I don't like veggies," mumbled Shelby.

"Good chefs like your dad and uncle can do amazing things with quality ingredients. Right, Levi?"

He shot her a grin. "I'm glad you think so, but I notice you're still not convinced I can outdo a coffee shop's brownies. They probably bring them in by the slab from a wholesaler."

She arched a brow at him. "Don't knock 'em 'til you've tried 'em."

Levi brought the car to a stop and flipped on the signal light. He leaned slightly across the console. "And don't knock mine. Challenge accepted. You'll see."

Heather thrilled at the intensity in his green eyes and

the whisper of his breath in that brief instant before he turned to check for traffic. What had just happened there? Was she imagining attraction rippling between them? Oh, she'd been feeling it since she'd caught that initial glimpse of him. Right about when she'd dropped the drill on her foot, calling his attention to her in the worst possible way. Maybe he'd finally gotten past that first impression.

In no time at all the three of them surrounded a table, treats in front of them.

Levi rubbed his hands together and picked up his plate. He passed the brownie in front of his nose.

Shelby giggled.

He winked at his niece then tipped his ear over the plate.

"Brownies don't talk, Uncle Levi."

"Well, you never know. I admit, I'd be a bit worried if it did. It would be a sure sign I shouldn't eat it, right?"

"Don't be silly. It's yummy." She took a big bite and grinned at him.

Levi nudged his niece with his elbow. "Yummy? Roll the taste around in your mouth. What does the texture feel like? How sweet is it? Sometimes they're so sweet you can't taste the flavors."

She offered a quizzical expression. "It's a brownie, and that's what it tastes like."

"Is it made from premium ingredients? Is it organic?" Levi raised his eyebrows at Shelby. "Don't just eat it. Analyze it."

Heather managed to keep her snicker contained. She'd be done with hers before he ever got a bite in. Procrastination might be part of the game, but it was fun to see him loosen up a little. She couldn't resist. "I hear organic-labeling is just an excuse for companies to charge more money."

Levi nodded. "Sometimes that's true."

Wait a minute. Had he really agreed? "And yet Mackies are big on organics for the resort."

He pointed his clean fork at her. "*Known* organics, hence the CSA. They can drive out to any of the farms that supply our kitchen and look at their operations. They don't trust the big agri-businesses like Jimmiesin Farms out in California."

"I thought organic had to pass a set of standards."

"They do. But many of the big companies are more concerned with the bottom line than they are about healthy soil and good management practices. They skirt the line as much as they can. It's money."

How many times had her father been so busy managing his investment firm that he'd been oblivious to his only child's life? Heather could count on one hand the number of times she'd had his undivided attention for more than five minutes. Levi was right. Dollar signs ruled the world.

Dad had paid for her degree in finance. She loved numbers, but she didn't want to fall into the trap that had swallowed him. What good was a life full of everything money could buy but empty of relationships, empty of love?

Shelby's voice brought her back to the coffee shop. "Well, what do you think, Uncle Levi?"

What, Heather had missed his first bite?

Levi chewed slowly, staring at the ceiling above Heather's head. "Hmm."

Who knew the man could be this much of a ham?

Heather couldn't help the grin that poked at the corners of her mouth.

His gaze shifted from Shelby to Heather. "Not bad. It's a bit dry and overly sweet, I think. And the nuts are too soft. But I've had worse."

"Too dry? I don't think so. And aren't brownies supposed to be sweet? They're a dessert."

Levi pointed his fork at her. This time, a few brown crumbs clung to it. "Sweet, yes. But not so sweet it overwhelms the other flavors."

He had a point, not that she'd let him know he'd scored it. She raised her eyebrows, catching Shelby's expectant look from the corner of her eye. "I can hardly wait to taste the perfect brownies, Chef Levi."

"Me, too," chimed in Shelby.

"You're on."

His gaze met Heather's for a long moment, but she didn't flinch. Didn't look away. He'd started it, and she was going to let him finish it. Whatever 'it' was.

LEVI CAME up the stairs from his basement bedroom to find Shelby sitting on the sofa.

"Do you think Mei and Yun will like their new clothes?" His niece stroked the pink panda pajamas she'd been unable to resist. As though neon pink pandas would make a little Chinese girl feel more at home.

Levi thought of the photos his brother had shared of the orphanage, and his heart twisted. "They will *love* their new clothes, and they'll love their new big sister, too."

What was he even thinking, craving his sterile life in Seattle? Why wouldn't he stay in Helena and help settle his new nieces? Help his older niece with the adjustments that were sure to come? There'd be all those surgeries, too. Jared and Aimee would need someone to help out with Shelby and Mei while they were busy with Yun.

Because he didn't have a job here, and he didn't want one. He was just filling in for his brother. Besides, he wanted the thrill of the Fireweed kitchen, especially the new location where the post-symphony crowd would stroll through in their tuxedos and gowns. Although, Helena had a symphony... and Jared and Aimee had two tickets they wouldn't be using for it in their bedroom upstairs.

"Uncle Levi?" Shelby refolded the pajamas and took out a pair of jeggings. Jean leggings. Who even knew that was a thing? But Heather and Shelby had agreed Mei and Yun each needed a pair.

"Hmm?"

"Why does Yun have a face like that? Can doctors really fix it?"

"Didn't Miss Heather show you pictures of what the kids looked like after surgery?"

She nodded, still looking pensive. "But how come? Is it because she's Chinese?"

"No. Some babies in America are born like that, too. It's just that doctors here perform surgery to fix it when the babies are really tiny, instead of four years old like Yun." He eyed his niece. "Don't you think her life will be so much better here with a fixed face and a family who loves her than staying in the orphanage the way she is now?"

To say nothing of being separated from Mei, her wee

champion. Jared had Dropboxed them a couple of videos of the two girls together, the crazy-glue bond between them evident. No wonder Jared and Aimee couldn't bear the thought of leaving Yun behind.

Shelby scrunched her nose. "Was I born like that? Did doctors fix me?"

"No, you weren't. But it can happen."

"So should I say thank you to God for letting me be beautiful?"

Levi managed to choke back the chuckle that wanted to escape. His niece was serious, and he needed to treat her question with respect. "God has given us many blessings, Shelby. It's always a good idea to show gratitude for them when we think of them."

She ducked her head. "Dear Jesus, thank You for making me beautiful." She hesitated. "Thank You for a mom and a dad and an uncle and for Miss Heather. Thank You for my friends Lila and Charlotte. Thank You for a house and not an orphanage."

Levi waited while she thought some more. How often did he list off the people and things he was thankful for? Not nearly enough.

"Thank you for pink parkas and jeggings and panda pajamas." She peeked up at Levi. "Can I have pink panda pajamas, too?"

"They didn't come in your size, remember?"

"Right." She scrunched her eyes closed again. "And thank You for dying for me so I could go to heaven someday. Because that's a blessing, too, right, Uncle Levi?"

His throat caught. "It is. Very definitely."

"Amen."

"Amen." He reached for the little girl — big girl, as she constantly reminded him — and she jumped into his lap. "You have a big heart, Shelby Ann."

She gave him a serious look. "It's big enough for Yun."

He hugged her. "I was glad to hear when you told your parents that. They were, too. You're not going to regret loving Yun."

"God wants us to love everyone."

"He does. And some people He wants us to love in a special way, like little sisters."

"Do you have a little sister?"

Levi chuckled. "You know I don't. Your dad is my older brother, remember? Our parents didn't have any other kids." That he knew about, anyway.

"I wonder if Miss Heather has a little sister."

He didn't even know. There were a lot of things he didn't know about Heather that he found himself wanting to learn. Even with a sore foot, she'd been a trooper today, making the day fun for all of them. Without her, he'd have come home in half an hour with a jacket for Shelby. With her, they'd spent several hours and come home with a few hundred dollars' worth of clothing for three girls. Good thing Jared had left him a fund.

But... Heather. His thoughts kept veering to her. Her dusky blond hair that looked so soft. The blue eyes that revealed her every mood. Her heart-shaped face and pink lips, her charming curves. Everything about her drew him, even her beauty, the very thing he should resist.

Except her focus on the superficial, but he'd managed to forget about that for hours at a time today. Was she deeper than he'd thought?

CHAPTER 8

*T*oday's lesson will take place in the dining room."
Heather surveyed the dozen students in her
etiquette classes for girls seven through fourteen.

Lila's face brightened. "Do we get a snack?"

"More than that. We are sampling an entire formal
dinner that the chef has prepared for us."

The girls' voices buzzed.

Heather held up her hand. "Excuse me, please.
Remember your manners. Remember to listen, to observe,
and to act like the young ladies you are."

Charlotte's hand shot up. "Chef Levi is a very good
cook."

"Yes, he is." More than a good cook. "And while that is
true, today's focus isn't you girls tasting the food. That's a
side benefit. Can anyone guess what the goal of this
class is?"

"Table manners?" asked Olivia Abercrombie from the
back of the group. She ruined it by snapping her gum.

"You are correct, Olivia. Now, please find a trash receptacle and deposit your gum."

Olivia rolled her eyes and stalked off.

When she returned, Heather led the girls into the dining room and stopped at a small table with one place setting. "Gather around, please. I'd like you to notice that there are more items on the table than you usually see at home. Three forks. Two spoons. Two glasses. As contestants, you need to know which to use when."

The girls eyed the gleaming china and crystal.

Good, she had their attention. "Our first formal dinner is next week on Friday at the Civic Center. It's for all the contestants and your families, as well as important dignitaries from the city of Helena and the press. Because it is Thanksgiving weekend, the chef will prepare a six-course dinner. You'll be expected to have a little of each, even if it is something you don't think you'll care for. And remember — at any moment, a reporter might be taking your photo for the Independent Record or a video clip for television. You don't want to be remembered as the girl whose nose wrinkled at the food."

Not like she'd once been recorded with egg dripping off her face. Literally.

"I have a question, Miss Heather." Olivia again.

"Yes?"

The girl's eyes glittered. "I hope it isn't going to be Mexican food because that's all the chef knows."

Heather's smile froze. "The menu consists of a six-course turkey dinner—"

"My mom and I are veg—"

"—with a vegetarian option."

"Well, fine then. So long as it isn't refried beans."

"That is enough, Olivia."

Olivia mumbled something to the girl next to her, who snickered.

"Miss Abercrombie. I said, that is quite enough. In this class, we treat everyone with respect. We don't turn our noses at the cuisines of other cultures. Ladies are gracious in every circumstance."

"Yes, Miss Heather."

"Thank you. Now let's talk about each item in this place setting. Then we'll each take a seat at the banquet tables and the waiters will serve us so you can practice. Any questions?"

The girls shook their heads.

Heather's gaze lingered on Shelby standing off to the side, eyes shooting daggers at Olivia. If only Levi's niece would keep her mouth shut and not retaliate.

LEVI SNAGGED a couple of chances to peek out of the kitchen and see how Heather was doing with Shelby and the others. He was dying of curiosity about how she prepared the girls for the pageant — focus on manners rather than looks was a good start — but he couldn't let himself get sidetracked. Dr. Mackie had specifically asked him to test the upcoming banquet menu for their youngest participants. It also provided the opportunity for the newer wait staff to practice before the big event.

He knew his food was up to par, but he'd never focused on pleasing children's palates before this.

"I think that's it for now." Manny carried in a tray of scraped-out dessert dishes. "Miss Heather is giving them a lecture on manners."

Levi chuckled. "Every banquet has its speeches. Gives the kitchen time to get caught up. Did you set out the candy and nut bowls?"

Manny nodded. "How about drinks for the kids? I know we offer coffee or tea for the adults with dessert, but it seems something is missing for the girls."

"Good call." Levi narrowed his gaze at the server. "We can easily do spiced apple cider for the banquet as a third option. It's something I can put on a back burner first thing in the morning, and it can simmer away all day."

"Cool." The young guy beamed. "I like that option myself. I'll see how much apple juice we have on hand." He turned and headed into the cooler.

Levi could try it out on Shelby tonight. Wonder what Heather would think of the cider? He shook his head. How did that thought keep popping into his head, time and time again, in the past few days? He'd never wondered what a woman thought before. At least not beyond his childhood when the questions had been why a mother would give her life to alcohol and ignore her children. Then, while he'd heard that most foster parents genuinely cared about kids in turmoil, he and Jared seemed to land the ones who were in it for the money.

What did he know about women? What made him think he could navigate a relationship, especially with a pretty one? He couldn't. Not a chance. But even less could he manage his niece without help while her parents were gone. The Mackies had assigned Heather to the job. Did they have a clue that he wouldn't be able to get his mind off her? Surely romance wasn't their intention. She was so distracting he'd had a jar of chicken broth poised over the vegetarian risotto before catching himself.

At least he *had* noticed it. Which made him worry about the things he might not have caught. And the more she was around, the easier it was to forget he was against all things pageantry.

A rustle at the door captured his attention, and he turned toward it.

Heather, wearing a periwinkle top that brought out the blue in her eyes, slim black pants, and cute heeled boots, a far cry from steel-toed boots or slippers and crutches.

"Yes? Any problems with the meal?" Drat, his voice sounded gruff. He cleared his throat.

Those blue eyes widened, and Heather's hand lifted to brush blond strands behind her ear. A dangling sapphire earring brushed her neck and caught his gaze. "No, it was fabulous. You outdid yourself, Levi. Even the pickiest eaters liked most of it."

Look at her eyes, man. Not the curves of the rest of her. Levi swallowed hard. "That's good."

"So, we're done now, and the girls are waiting for their rides."

He looked at her blankly, trying to bring his mind into the here-and-now.

"I know you're off your regular schedule today, so I wasn't sure what you wanted me to do with Shelby. If you're going to be long, she can come up to my place."

Levi glanced over to where Opal was well into dinner prep for the staff and guests. Then he took in the remainder of the kitchen. "I'm not quite done with cleanup. Maybe half an hour?" He couldn't ask the evening staff to do it. He'd made the mess.

"Sure. You know where to find us, then."

He did.

She turned and strolled out of the kitchen and, like a hound on a scent, he followed her then leaned in the doorway while she paused to survey the waiting girls.

Shelby's friends Charlotte and Lila stood on either side of the chair where Shelby slouched, a scowl on her face.

"Last time I sang *Away in a Manger*," Lila announced. "Charlotte played piano. Do you play piano, Shelby?"

His niece shook her head, still glowering.

That was an unusual look on her.

"There are lots of kinds of talents," Charlotte put in. "Emily tap dances. She won Little Miss Snowflake. We didn't, but it was still fun."

"I can't tap dance, either. I do cartwheels."

"I keep trying," Lila said. "But I always fall over. See?" Her attempt landed her in a giggling heap on the floor.

Levi's gaze slid back to his niece. "What happened to Shelby?" he asked quietly. "Even her friends can't cheer her up."

Heather bit her lip and shook her head. "Olivia Abercrombie happened to her. That girl is taking too many lessons from her mother."

"Like what?" All he remembered were the woman's accusations about meat. In fact, he'd mentioned that — removing the tone — when he'd discussed the banquet menu with Dr. and Mrs. Mackie. They'd agreed he should include a full vegetarian option.

"She's just rude. That's all."

Levi set his hand on Heather's forearm as she turned away.

She halted, staring at his hand, before slowly raising her gaze to his.

"Heather, what did she say?" He was going to ignore the feel of her soft skin beneath his fingers.

She hesitated. "Nothing you need to worry about. It's within the pageant, and I'll deal with it."

"Heather. *What did she say?* Because Shelby looks devastated. And that *is* something that concerns me."

"Fine. She made nasty remarks about the vegetarian option probably being refried beans since you're Mexican and then later—"

"She *what?*"

"See, that's why I didn't want to tell you. I handled it, okay?"

Levi glared at Heather, feeling her muscles tense beneath his fingers. He should remove his hand. Instead, he slid it down until he captured her fingers in his. "You said, then later. What more happened?"

"Just some stuff about Chinese kids. She used insulting words."

His fingers tightened and his gaze bored into hers. "I'll have a word with—"

"No." Heather yanked her hand away. "It is pageantry business, and I'll deal with it. If Olivia doesn't straighten up, she'll be out of the competition. There's no room for girls who don't respect others."

He snorted. "You think that's enough punishment?" Because he didn't.

"Yes, I do. Her little sister won the Little Miss category last year. Trust me, Olivia doesn't want Emily better than her at anything. She fully intends to win Junior Miss, and she'll do anything she can to stay in it once she realizes how serious I am."

Levi shook his head. How little he understood women and pageantry. "That doesn't even make sense."

Heather's hands landed on her hips as she leaned in a little. "As a veteran of twenty-seven pageants that I did not win, I totally believe Olivia will toe the line. She's competitive."

Wait. What? She'd *lost* twenty-seven competitions? But... "How many did you win?"

Her lips tightened as she looked down. "None." And she turned away.

He grasped her arm again. "None? Are you serious? But you teach—"

"I'm perfectly aware." Her eyes shot fire. "Don't think Priscilla Abercrombie hasn't reminded me how unqualified I am."

"But you embody—" Everything he'd always hated about pageantry until he'd started getting to know her.

Her raised eyebrows above glittering blue eyes stopped him. "What do you think, Levi Esteban? That I'm a silly female who thinks of nothing but clothes and makeup?"

He hadn't thought that since about their third interaction. He shook his head. Obviously, it was best to keep his mouth zipped with his thoughts locked inside.

"Because I'm not. I'm a college graduate who spent five years working with Habitat for Humanity. I've broken a nail or two in my day and lived to tell the tale. I may have come from privilege, but it hasn't ruled my life, so I'll thank you not to jump to conclusions about me, any more than Olivia Abercrombie should jump to conclusions about your cooking mastery."

The only conclusion he wanted to jump to right then was the taste of her lips. But she was right. Jumping without thought wasn't going to do either of them any good.

He finally managed some words. "Point taken. I'll pick up Shelby in a little while." And he turned and reentered the kitchen.

ay to push him away, Heather. Just when it seemed he might be getting interested, give him a shove. Make sure he knows you're a loser.

She'd barely slept for three nights for the hours tossing and turning. Lack of true rest hadn't helped her foot complete its healing, either. The swelling kept her out of cute shoes, and the miserable rain kept her on crutches, since she couldn't get her waterproof boots on, and a soaked slipper was no fun at all.

She wasn't working enough hours to justify what Grizzly Gulch was paying her, but Mrs. Mackie waved off her concerns. Now she felt like she was taking advantage of them, even though she wasn't. Not really.

The past three days, Levi was back to texting when he was off work so Shelby could meet him downstairs. The little girl had recovered from Olivia's taunts and was back to skipping and flipping through life.

That didn't help Heather's frame of mind by much. She just wanted to growl.

A gentle tap sounded after lunch on Friday, and she glared at the door from across the room. The footsteps coming down the old building's creaky corridor had been light, so it wasn't Levi. Not that it would be, anyway.

She hobbled over to the door and opened it to Kristen. "Oh. Hi."

"Hi yourself." Kristen grinned and peered past her. "Can I come in? Is this a good time?"

Heather stepped back and tried to remember her manners. "Would you like some tea? Coffee?"

"You know me. I'd love a coffee." Kristen shrugged out of her raincoat and removed her rain boots. "It's sure miserable out there."

And in here. Nothing but gray. Heather turned on the kettle. "I don't have all the fancy stuff for what I know you drink."

Kristen laughed. "I can handle coffee with just cream on occasion. It doesn't always have to be a sugar-free white chocolate mocha with a shot of peppermint and no whip."

Heather managed a grin. "Well, I've got the 'no whip' down pat."

She felt Kristen's eyes on her as the water heated then she poured it into the French press. "Something wrong, Heather?"

Figured. "Just... life. It's nothing that won't pass." As soon as Aimee and Jared returned and Levi left for parts unknown. And Olivia Abercrombie grew up a little. And Heather's mother accepted her as a valid human even without a crown.

She pushed the plunger down in the coffee maker. Maybe her mother was more of her problem than she'd thought, what with Thanksgiving looming less than a week away now.

Kristen rummaged in the fridge for cream and poured a splash into each cup as Heather filled them with coffee. Kristen eyed her. "Want to talk about it?"

Not really?

Heather pointed toward the love seat at the other end of the space. "I'm sure you had something else in mind when you dropped by. What's up?"

Her friend curled up in the corner, tucking her feet under her. "I've been meaning to catch you in the dining room the past couple of days, but you always seem to be in a hurry."

Heather took a sip of her coffee.

Kristen sighed. "Okay, there are a couple of things. One, I wanted to confirm the entries for the pageants. Todd's agency will send the program to the printers on Monday, if you could check it over."

Had that been in her email? Seemed like it. "I can do that."

"Secondly, I chatted with Aimee on Skype yesterday. I'm sure you know things are moving forward with adopting the second little girl. My parents are super excited to pay for Yun's surgery."

The Mackies had more money than they knew what to do with, it seemed. But they were always ready to embrace a new charitable project. "It must be a load off Aimee's mind."

"Yes. But, of course, that's not enough for my parents."

Heather raised her eyebrows above her coffee mug. "Oh?"

"Aimee and Jared have a room set aside for a nursery, but Beijing called before they were ready, and they didn't have time to get it decorated. Plus, it only has one bed, one dresser, etcetera. So my parents want to get the room painted and welcoming for two little girls."

"That's very thoughtful."

Kristen laughed. "Sometimes they seem a little pushy, but I begged Mom to let me broach it with Aimee, and she and Jared are super relieved." She shrugged.

What did that have to do with Heather? She wanted to ask, but didn't dare. Patience.

"I was wondering, seeing as how you and Levi looked all cozy on Sunday, if you'd like to take on buying furniture and accessories. Maybe with him and Shelby? Mom will give you a preloaded card, so you wouldn't need to worry about spending money and waiting for reimbursement."

"No, I don't think that's a good idea. Levi and I... well, let's just say that isn't working out."

"Oh, no." Kristen set her mug down, a look of dismay crossing her face. "Are you sure it isn't just growing pains? I think all relationships have those."

"Pretty sure not."

"What happened? If I'm not being too snoopy."

Heather was in this far, and with Marisa and Jase in Nicaragua, she didn't really have anyone else to confide in. "It's just, he's got it all together, and I'm a mess. I might have told him about the twenty-seven pageants I didn't win. He already knows I'm a klutz because I dropped that stupid drill on my foot when I first saw him. He—"

"Wait. Back up a sec. The drill was because of him?"

Heat rose up Heather's face. This was exactly why she

shouldn't confide in anyone. She couldn't trust herself to filter effectively.

Kristen leaned forward, hands clasped in her lap. "Do tell me more."

"CAN we go shopping with Miss Heather again? Charlotte told me that her grandma said Miss Heather is going to buy some things for Mei and Yun's bedroom on Black Friday, and I want to go." Shelby bounced on the balls of her feet in front of Levi.

He'd heard the same rumor. When he'd expressed his unease with the Mackies' generosity to his brother, Jared had laughed. "They mean well, and we're so thankful for them. They've done as much and more for dozens if not hundreds of other families. Who do you think encouraged us to go for international adoption to begin with?"

It still bugged Levi, even though Jared said it was because the two of them had been raised without a family. If Mackies wanted to be grandparents to Jared's kids, it was fine with him and Aimee. Who was Levi to come between Jared and his new wealthy family? It didn't nullify the bond between the brothers.

"Uncle Levi? Can I?"

He blinked at the eight-year-old. "Uh... on Black Friday? I don't think so. That's early and crazy both."

"But it's for my sisters." Shelby angled her head to the side. "Will you come, too? You could protect me from crazy."

If only. He smothered a laugh. "Oh, I don't think so. I

don't know anything about what little girls need, and shopping with the crazies is more than I can handle."

"Silly! You're taking care of me just fine. You and Miss Heather."

He tweaked her nose. "You're a bigger little girl." But wouldn't the additions be just as much his nieces as this one was? Blood wasn't everything. As Jared tried to explain about the Mackies and how they'd welcomed them in. Some families were born, some were built, and some were a mix.

"Besides, you told Miss Heather you'd make brownies last time we went shopping, and you haven't."

So much for his hope everyone had forgotten. "It's only been a week, and we've been really busy. Maybe after Thanksgiving." A long, long time after Thanksgiving.

"Charlotte says—"

He was getting mighty tired of those words.

"—they're going to paint the walls pink. She said on Friday, so you can help."

"No need to wait for me. Someone else can do it."

Shelby's lip protruded in a pout. "How come you're no fun?"

Levi raised his eyebrows. "Being fun isn't my job. Taking care of you is my job. Being as good a chef as your dad is my job. Both of those are full time. That's all I've got time for right now."

The girl's arms crossed her chest as she stared up at him. Eight, going on fourteen.

"I'll talk to Mrs. Mackie tomorrow." If only to find out why he hadn't been kept in the loop.

"Yay!"

"As for shopping... I don't think so."

"But I like being with Miss Heather. A lot."

So did Levi. Or he would, if he allowed himself to. "She's nice."

Shelby's face brightened. "You should—"

He held up a hand. "No, I shouldn't. Whatever you were about to say, no."

"But she's sad, not happy like when we went shopping. She said I was lucky to have a mom and dad who love me so much, because her mom and dad don't. And she doesn't even have one sister or brother."

Heather had no siblings and a rocky relationship with her parents? Why didn't he know this already? Maybe because he'd shut down conversation before they'd gotten anywhere near personal things.

"Shelby, remember I don't really live in Helena. When your parents come back from China, your dad will get his job back, and I'll go back to Seattle." Hopefully with the promotion to the new location.

"But you can't."

Man, now it looked like tears would gush out any minute. Girls. "Pumpkin, I have to. I need a job, and this one is your dad's." He held up a hand to forestall another attack. "Besides, you won't need me anymore."

She launched at him, wrapping both arms around his middle so tightly he nearly lost his balance. "But I do need you. And you can make Miss Heather smile."

Levi patted her shoulder. "We'll let God do that, okay?"

Shelby's head tilted as she looked up at him. "I'll ask Him to, but Mommy says sometimes we have to help God when we know how."

Out of the mouth of babes. "Off you go."

She gave him a long look then disappeared up the stairs, her hand trailing on the banister.

Levi sank onto a stool at the kitchen island and rested his head in his hands. Was his niece right? Was God asking him to help Heather smile? Because a smiling Heather meant a smiling Levi, and that could only go one direction.

A direction that wasn't the Fireweed in Seattle.

CHAPTER 10

*H*eather dumped the armload of bags on the floor of Aimee and Jared's entryway.

"I'll get the rest of them," said Kristen from behind her. "You should get off that foot. I can't believe someone stomped on it trying to grab that lotus flower bedding you already had in your hands."

Heather winced. "Black Friday for you." But the greedy shopper's pointy heel hadn't done the bridge of her sore foot any good. Who knew she should wear steel-toed boots in the department store at six a.m.?

"Hey, you're back!" yelled Kristen's husband down the stairs then appeared, holding a paintbrush. "Did you get everything? Need a hand?"

"I've got it, hon," Kristen called back. "Just one more load, I think. Hey, you look great in pink."

Heather couldn't help laughing as Todd looked down at his black T-shirt with assorted pink smears, and shrugged. "Perils of being a girl dad. Levi doesn't have a drop on him."

Levi would make a great girl dad. Or boy dad. Heather's

heart squeezed. Not only was she spending the next few hours with him — well, him and Kristen and Todd — but she'd promised Kristen she'd give him a chance. That hadn't been easy to say, but talking to him would be like ripping off an adhesive bandage, right? She'd get the words out then the whole thing would be over. Her speech wouldn't change his opinion of her, but at least she'd have said her piece.

Only — please, God — not in front of Kristen and Todd.

"Come on up. We just got started." Todd disappeared into the room at the head of the stairs.

Heather dug through the bags for the one containing her painting clothes then changed in the powder room off the entry before limping up the stairs. By then, Kristen had the rest of their shopping in the house and was shrugging off her dripping coat. Had there ever been such a wet and dreary Thanksgiving weekend?

She paused in the hallway, taking in the stacked furniture, before entering the room. Levi ran a paintbrush, loaded with pink, along the ceiling. No tape? She held her breath lest she cause him to smudge. When his brush came away, she clasped her hands. "Wow, good job. You're a pro at this."

He flashed her a grin that could've melted her socks off. Maybe he wasn't mad at her anymore. "Painted houses for a couple of years."

She'd wielded a brush some with Habitat for Humanity, too, but she'd felt more comfortable swinging a hammer.

"Good thing we have him," joked Todd. "I asked Rob if he'd help, and he said he'd rather corral wild horses. So, we dropped off Charlotte, Liam and Shelby at their house. He may wish he'd worded it differently."

"Is Bren really up to a houseful of kids?" Heather was no expert on pregnancy, but Bren didn't have her usual glow and energy these days, and the baby wasn't due for another six weeks or so.

Todd dipped a roller into the paint tray. "Rob said he'd keep them all entertained. He had a billion younger cousins, so he knows the tricks and games. I'm sure he'll call if he needs something."

"What can I do to help?" Heather pointed at the clean, straight line separating the would-be pink wall from the white ceiling. "I can't do *that*, for sure."

"Nothing on a ladder." Kristen came up beside her. "Some hostile deal-snatcher stomped on Heather's foot."

A quick frown crossed Levi's face as he stepped off the low stepladder.

He was probably worried he'd have to carry her somewhere again. Heat burned up Heather's face. "I'm fine." Well, not right then, but she would be. In a few weeks. Hopefully.

"You sure? Because you don't have to help."

Her chin lifted. "I am perfectly capable."

"Grab a roller, then. The closet needs painting."

"I'll go in there," Kristen said quickly. "That way no one will have to look at my lousy skills. You follow along behind Levi."

"I'll do the upper walls, and you can get the lower," Todd suggested. "Keep you off a ladder."

Guess everyone made her decisions for her. "Fine." It

wasn't like her foot didn't hurt. She was so sick of the pain already.

"Did you get everything on the list?" asked Todd.

Heather nodded as she picked up a roller. "Bedding, curtains, another bed and dresser — they had the same style on sale, so that's a bonus — and some accessories." She shot a guilty glance toward the closet, where Kristen brushed paint into the corner. "And, um, we might've bought more clothes."

"Might've?" Todd laughed.

She looked up at Levi as he edged his brush around the window frame.

He paused, watching her. "Thank you." He bit his lip, but his green eyes didn't leave hers, as he made a room-shaped circle in the air with his brush. "You didn't have to do all this."

He was right. Mackies weren't paying her to paint, at least that she knew of. "I wanted to. Aimee is my friend, too."

Levi nodded and reloaded his brush.

Man, the guy could clam up faster than anyone she'd ever met. He wasn't going to make today easy. Still, she'd promised Kristen. Okay, it wasn't only that. So what if she was a little forward? He was leaving in a few weeks... unless he decided to stay. What did she have to lose?

Heather rolled paint beside the window. "Have you and Jared always been close?"

Levi glanced at her. "He's seven years older than me, so not really. But he always looked out for me when he could."

That was a strange answer. She studied him until he looked back.

He took a deep breath. "We were put in foster care when I was five. Together, at first, but it didn't last. The first time we were moved, they separated us. Said they didn't have a home for us together. After a few years, Jared had complained enough times they reunited us, but when he aged out, it got worse again." He shrugged. "It's just how it was."

Tears pooled in Heather's eyes. "How awful. What happened to your parents?"

His jaw stiffened as he brushed. "We never knew our fathers, and our mother loved alcohol more than she loved us."

No wonder trust came so hard for him. "My mom loved prestige more than she loved me."

His eyebrows rose as he glanced her way.

"If you think twenty-seven beauty pageants were *my* idea, you'd be dead wrong. It was all my mother. She wanted a crown on my head more than anything in the world."

"That's crazy."

"Yeah, well, it's still true."

"Why put all that on a kid? Did she enter pageants herself?"

Heather shook her head. "She made sure I remembered she didn't have the advantages I had, growing up. She longed to be considered beautiful all her life. It was my job to turn heads in her place."

LEVI SET the brush down and turned toward her. "You have got to be kidding. What mother in her right mind...?" He couldn't finish the sentence.

Her pretty blue eyes met his for a second, and he barely caught her grimace. "Who said anything about her right mind?"

"I just remembered something we needed to do downstairs!" Kristen caught Todd's hand and dragged him out of the room.

Good people, the O'Briens. Kristen's parents, too. Everyone surrounded Jared and Aimee with love and acceptance. They must know Jared was a foster kid. Why had his brother turned out open and trusting, while Levi held back?

No more. He needed to take a chance. He needed to see Heather's smile again.

Levi stepped closer. "But she must be beautiful, because you are." If she'd been adopted, she'd have said so, wouldn't she?

"Do... do you really think so?"

"Absolutely. I don't know what all they look for in a winner, but they're crazy to have passed you by." Unless a pageant had been rigged. "You're pretty, and you're smart, and you're nice to everyone, and... do I need to go on?" Because, now that he'd gotten started, he could.

Her grin slid sideways. "And I'm clumsy. Don't forget that."

"I don't think you are. Dropping the drill was an accident. It could happen to anyone." His mind replayed the incident from a few weeks back. The wide-eyed look on her face before the drill slipped. Could it have been...? Nah. Not because of him.

"I was... distracted."

His heart hammered in his chest. "Distracted by what?"

"You." Her gaze flicked to his then away. "Aimee told me you were really hot, and I wanted to see for myself."

No. Way. "You were there on purpose?"

She nodded, just barely.

Levi took the roller out of her hand and set it on the tray. He could hardly hear his own voice over the thudding in his chest, remembering his first glimpse of her. "What did you think?"

"That she was kind of right."

This couldn't be real. No one had hurled insults at his looks, but only his eyes garnered positive remarks. Levi tilted her chin. "I don't know what to say."

A glimmer of a grin appeared then vanished. "My mother taught me the appropriate response is 'thank you'."

Somehow he hadn't stopped touching her. He needed to do that, but his hand didn't get the message. Instead, his fingers traced her jaw. "In that case, thank you." He took a deep breath. "Your beauty goes so much deeper than your face. You're one of the most caring people I've ever met. Granted, my life has been a bit jaded."

Her blue eyes locked onto his, and he felt like he could read through to her soul. Like she'd opened it up for him to see. What was she seeing in his eyes? What if she was seeing too much, more than he was willing to share?

Tempting as it was to lean down those few inches and taste her lips, it was too soon. Much too soon... and besides, there was Seattle.

Levi dropped his hand with a rueful grin. "Shelby and I

are going to see the Parade of Lights tonight. I hear it's amazing. Want to come with us?"

"That would be... sure. I'd like that."

"Great," said Kristen from the doorway. "Not to interrupt or anything, but can we finish painting this room? Because Todd just ordered a pizza delivery to Bren and Rob's for 4:30 so we can all get downtown on time."

Heather glanced toward the door then back at Levi, a tiny grin poking at the corners of her mouth. "Friends," she muttered.

He chuckled. "Sure. We can get back to work. As soon as we have the first coat on, let's drop by the dining hall. Nella is setting out rolls and cold cuts at noon. Then on to touch-ups."

"I just tossed a load of the bedding into Aimee's washer," added Kristen. "Whenever we're ready to bring the furniture back in, we can finish everything up."

Levi shook his head. "Not today. There's no rush, and I'd like to let the walls dry more thoroughly before we start bumping things into them. Maybe next weekend."

Kristen stuck her lips out in a pout, and Heather laughed. "They won't be back with the girls until just before Christmas, so Levi's right. We have plenty of time. And I think Shelby will want to be part of setting up."

Plenty of time. Maybe for finishing up Mei and Yun's bedroom, but was there enough time to see where this new thing with Heather might go? What if he stepped out of the running in Seattle only to find out they weren't suited after all? Or he couldn't find a job here? Helena had plenty of restaurants, but nothing close to the vision the Fireweed's investors had. He wanted to be part of that.

He glanced at Heather as she spread pink paint a few feet away from him.

Did he want that vision more than he wanted a relationship with Heather? He didn't have long to figure that out.

Not long at all.

CHAPTER 11

*A*re you girls ready to go out there and wow everyone?" Heather peeked around the door into the Helena Civic Center ballroom. "Looks like every seat is taken. All the city dignitaries have come to get a glimpse of what the new season of the Snowflake Pageant will hold."

Across the ballroom, the door to the catering kitchen swung as a black-garbed waiter exited with a tray of sparkling glasses. Somewhere beyond it, Levi and Opal worked in tandem to produce a banquet for over four hundred guests. They'd done all the prep they could back at the resort, since the Civic Center kitchen wasn't designed for full service.

Shelby caught Heather's attention as she dashed across the ready room and twirled into a cartwheel, her long brown hair fanning like a halo as she rotated. Charlotte and Lila giggled.

Heather needed to focus. She turned to the group of ten to twelve year olds. "How about you? Any questions or comments before we go out?"

One of the girls who hadn't been in the etiquette classes slid a side glance toward Olivia Abercrombie, who stood giggling with her clique of friends, then turned her gaze back to Heather. The girl looked pale, her eyes large.

Heather crossed the room and slipped her arm around the girl's shoulders. "It's okay, sweetie," she murmured. "Just be yourself. It isn't all about winning, remember? It's about stretching ourselves. Gaining confidence."

The girl sent a sidelong look at Olivia, who glanced over her way and smirked.

"She's just playing mind games. It isn't only about winning the crown. Even though this is sometimes called a beauty pageant, it isn't all about being pretty, either."

Olivia sauntered over. "It's a good thing you think that, Miss Heather, because my mom told me that you have never won a single competition. How will you feel when I'm a winner, and you never were?"

Heather straightened and kept her smile in place. "I've been a winner in many ways." Not that the girl would count being named Miss Congeniality. "It really isn't all about the contest. This is only preparation for real life."

Did she honestly believe that? Because she had entered so many pageants it might be hard to tell from her track record. She could always blame it on her own mother.

Stand up straighter. Pop your hip out. Toss a smile over your shoulder as you turn away, hand on your hip. Oh, Heather Jeannine, did you forget the white strips for your teeth again? Then there was the pageant when a four-year-old Heather had a bad cold and sneezed, blowing a glob of snot across the room. She had burst into tears and run off the platform, where her mother had yelled about how humiliated she'd been. It had always been all about Mom, not about Heather.

She tried to block the memory of her almost-win in L.A. out of her mind. Competition did crazy things to girls, but there'd been that protest as the contestants were ushered from the bus to the event center's back door. She'd got an egg on her cheek, an elbow in her eye... and lost her edge.

Thankfully, no one protested the Miss Snowflake. She didn't have to go through that again.

Heather focused on the girls clustering around her and took a deep breath. "I'd like to remind you that we're working on our manners and skills through the pageantry classes. The goal isn't to prove who is best at everything, contrary to what it seems. Sure, the tiara is a nice thing to win. But the real goal is for every girl in this room to learn new skills, to gain confidence, and to do her best. This is what we've been working toward in the past two months during our lessons. You've all learned so much about poise and public speaking since we began meeting together."

She looked Olivia in the eye, which wasn't hard to do as the preteen was almost as tall as she was. "You've all been assigned to me to become ladies. That's the real goal here. So let's not forget what we've learned. How we treat others is vital, and an insolent attitude is not acceptable."

The little girls jabbered in the corner as Heather fingered the hem of her sapphire blue dress. She held a hope that it would catch Levi's eye. Was she just as shallow as Olivia Abercrombie? "We'll get the entrance signal any minute now. Please line up in the correct order. Remember what to do when your name is announced?"

"Our group is first." Shelby bounced on the balls of her feet.

A tap sounded at the door and Heather scurried over to open it.

"Ready?" asked Kristen.

"We are." Heather turned to the girls. "Little Misses? Over here, in line. Junior Misses, right behind them."

The girls shifted into the order they'd practiced.

Heather peeked through the door. Jase's camera pointed her way from a tripod, ready for the contestants' parade to the platform.

"Please welcome our Little Misses!" boomed Dr. Mackie through the microphone. "Our first contestant is Miss Charlotte O'Brien."

Charlotte, her red-gold hair arranged into loose ringlets, walked across the floor and up the steps to the platform where she took her place under the spotlight with a curtsy.

"Miss Charlotte O'Brien is eight years old and is a resident of Helena, Montana. She attends school at..."

Heather tuned out the Master of Ceremonies and beckoned to Emily. The contest was on.

USUALLY LEVI DIDN'T MIND BEING unable to see into the dining room. Tonight, however, he wished he had a glimpse. How was Shelby doing? How about Heather?

"How's it going out there, Manny?" All Levi knew was that every one of the six courses had been served.

"Good, Chef." Manny set a large tray covered with empty dessert dishes on the counter beside the dishwasher and gave the new hire a nudge. "Better get on those, buddy." He winked.

Levi peeked over the swinging door. He'd scouted the ballroom during setup, well before the doors had opened to the public. He knew exactly where Heather's place card had been set. The realization that Heather was growing on him — or something a bit more serious — had unsettled him, but in a good way. He couldn't ignore the attraction anymore, no matter how hard he tried.

There she was at a round table with Shelby beside her. Heather's gorgeous blond hair was stacked on her head. Even from here he could see the sapphire earrings gleaming against her pale skin. He'd like to kiss that exposed neck. Nuzzle it. Taste it.

Dr. Mackie said something — Levi had no clue what — and Heather laughed along with the others in the dining room as she leaned closer to Shelby. Her arm slid around the back of his niece's chair, and Shelby grinned up at her.

Mouth dry, Levi turned back to the kitchen. Really, all the cooking was done, and Opal had already slipped out. The guys didn't need him to help clean up the mess that remained.

"Hey, Manny? Do you need me for anything?"

"Nah, go ahead, Chef. I know you're anxious to see how your niece enjoyed the opening pageant."

"If you're sure you don't mind..."

"Go for it."

Levi ducked into the restroom in the corridor and glanced in the mirror. He combed back his hair. Good thing he'd worn a black shirt and black pants under his chef's tunic. He looked respectable even without a full tux, didn't he? He grinned to himself. No one was going to kick the chef out.

He carried a folding chair as he edged between the tables then popped it open between Heather and Kristen. "Do you mind if I join you?" he whispered.

Heather startled as he took his seat. A slow smile creased her cheeks. "No, of course you are welcome."

"Good to know." He leaned closer to Shelby. "Hey, how did it go?"

Shelby glanced at him, her eyes glittering in excitement. "This is so much fun!"

Now why wasn't he surprised to hear that? Levi grinned and nodded to Heather. "She seems really into it." And she was still a happy, active kid. Huh.

Heather smiled. "She sure does."

Dr. Mackie sat down at a nearby table, and a woman dressed in a glittering evening gown stepped to the microphone. "Welcome to the third annual revived Snowflake Pageant."

Why had he wanted to come sit out in the dining room again? He'd made a point of being against all this stuff... to a point he didn't want Heather — or anyone else — to ever discover. But when he looked around at the female contingent he was currently with, he wasn't so sure why it'd once seemed such a big deal.

He glanced at Heather next to him. She'd turned to listen to the speaker, which gave him a really good profile view of her pretty face and pert nose. How much makeup was she wearing? He'd laughed at women's makeup before, but it wasn't as unsettling as he'd expected. After all, Heather could swing a hammer or a paintbrush and be as tough as she needed to be. Seeing this very feminine side of her stirred something deep within him.

It was only that he was thankful for her help, right? No, there was definitely more. He shook his head slightly just as everyone around him laughed at something the speaker said. It was too late to pretend Heather hadn't captured his attention. He was pretty sure she felt the same way, after yesterday's excursion to the Parade of Lights.

Was he ready to find out, for sure? Could he do things differently, this time? Scenarios of the various responses she might make ran through his mind throughout the entire speech. He didn't hear a word of it that he'd remember later. Soon Dr. Mackie took the microphone again and thanked everyone for coming.

Levi turned to Heather. "Do you have plans for the rest of the evening?" He held his breath.

She looked up at him, her blue eyes sparkling. "I was just going to go back to my rooms and put on a chick flick."

Levi swallowed hard. Now or never. "Do you have something Shelby and I might enjoy? You could bring it over."

"I could come up with something, I'm sure." Heather looked at him with her eyebrows raised.

"Only if you want to." He held her gaze.

"What are we going to watch?" Shelby twirled beside their chairs.

Heather kept looking straight at Levi. "I, um, I don't know. How about the Princess Bride?"

"I love that movie!"

Levi glanced at Shelby. "Why don't you find your coat and get ready to go? I'll check in with the kitchen one last time."

Shelby scampered off. Levi turned back to Heather. "Is this okay with you?"

"Yes." Trusting blue eyes looked up at him. "Though I'm not sure what's going on."

"I'm not sure either," he said, catching her hand. "But I'm willing to find out if you are."

And he really was.

CHAPTER 12

*I*t felt different, sitting in Aimee and Jared's house with Levi. She hadn't been often, for all she thought of Aimee as her friend.

"Do you want some more popcorn?" Levi glanced at her where she sat at the other end of the sectional sofa.

"No, that's okay. I should probably be heading back to Tomah House soon." There, that tossed the ball firmly in his court.

"Want to wait a few minutes? I'll send Shelby to get ready for bed then we can talk for a bit. If you want."

Heather tried to look away from Levi's mesmerizing green eyes, but it was difficult. Was he really thinking what she'd been hoping he would start thinking? It seemed like he was interested in her, but that couldn't be. He just wanted to thank her for all the time she spent with his niece, right? His signals had been mixed for weeks.

But not with that look on his face. Suddenly she could scarcely get her breath. "I can. Sure. I could stay a little longer."

Shelby yawned and stretched as she levered up off her spot on the floor. "I'm so tired. Thanks for a great movie, Miss Heather. And for that cheesy popcorn, Uncle Levi."

The little girl went up the stairs and shut her bedroom door. She'd come back out again in a minute, right? She'd need to brush her teeth and use the restroom.

What should Heather do in the meanwhile? Spend a few minutes speculating what might happen? How serious was Levi about this move forward? Would he retreat again? Because she wasn't sure she could handle that.

He rose, gathered the empty popcorn bowls, and took them to the kitchen across the open floor plan. Apparently that was *his* way of dealing with the wait time. But what did he want to talk about with her? They'd had fun painting the room yesterday with Kristen and Todd. The parade along Last Chance Gulch had felt like a date, even with Shelby and hundreds of other people crowded around them.

And tonight he'd joined them for the closing parts of the banquet. Had it been just because of his niece, or was her heart correct in that there was something more? There had to be more. He hadn't invited anyone else over for a movie.

Shelby darted across the corridor upstairs and raced to the bathroom. Sounds of splashing ensued, and soon she bounded downstairs to give a hug to Levi.

"Good night, Uncle Levi." Shelby gave him a big squeeze around the middle. Then she dashed over to Heather and snuggled up beside her on the sofa. "Good night, Miss Heather."

Heather wrapped her arm around the little girl and gave

her a hug. "Good night, sweetie." She smoothed Shelby's hair. "Have a great sleep."

"I will!" Shelby bounced off the sofa and scurried up to her room.

Heather glanced over to see Levi busy in the kitchen. Now what? There couldn't possibly be much more for him to do tidying up the popcorn. She crossed to the island and slid onto a stool. "I think she had a good day."

Levi paused with a damp cloth in his hand. "I think she did." He wrung out the dishcloth and draped it over the faucet. Then he stood across the island looking at her.

This was awkward. Maybe she should just go home now. Maybe she shouldn't have agreed to come at all. But how could she make her escape when he had specifically asked her to stay?

Silence reigned for a few moments. If Shelby was still bouncing around upstairs, Heather couldn't hear her. She closed her eyes.

"Can I get you something to drink?" asked Levi.

Heather's eyes sprang open. "I, um, sure. Maybe a cup of herbal tea, if you have it."

He put on a kettle and opened the cupboard. "Is mint okay?" he asked.

"That sounds good."

Now if only she could get through what remained of this evening without making a fool of herself.

WHAT WAS he doing with a woman in his brother's house? It wasn't like they were unchaperoned, not with a little girl upstairs, but the question was deeper than that. How had he decided that getting to know Heather would be a good idea?

He took his time preparing the tea. He could see the questions on Heather's face as she watched him from the other side of the island. What was he going to say to her? "Sorry I don't have any brownies made." Oh, man, that just sounded lame.

"That's okay." She smiled at him. "You might have another chance or two to remedy that."

A leading comment if he'd ever heard one. Levi cringed. He was in it bad. Only three weeks of having her in and out of his life was enough to make him realize he wanted to know her better. It was crazy to get involved. His future was in Seattle. So was his job. He didn't do relationships anymore.

His heart didn't care.

He set two cups of tea on the granite island. "I should have asked if you wanted cream or sugar."

Heather rose and rounded the island. "I can help myself. At least if you have some honey in the house."

"I can get it." Suddenly he seemed way too close to Heather. Close enough to smell her sweet perfume. Close enough to reach out and touch the arm of her soft-looking sweater. The blue matched her eyes and the dangling earrings that grazed her alluring neck. He was a goner. "I'll get it for you." The words came out hoarse.

She looked up at him and her lips parted. He forced his gaze back to her eyes. But even that wasn't good enough. Those blue eyes, so trusting, so curious. He was bound to disappoint her. He wiped his clammy hands down the sides of his blue jeans — he'd taken time to change while she'd stopped by her own apartment to change and pick up the movie. It didn't matter what she wore. She was beautiful.

"Do you really think so?"

Did he think what? Had he said that out loud? How much had actually been verbal?

"Heather. You are beautiful." This time he knew that he was saying it out loud. And it didn't seem such a negative thing, after all. Hopefully his niece wasn't crouched at the head of the stairs, listening. For better or for worse, the words hung in the air between them. They meant even more today than they had yesterday. "Not only that, but your spirit is just as beautiful as your face."

He stretched his hand and touched her hair. Trailed his fingers down her throat to her shoulder. Just a whisper.

Her eyes widened, but she stood still. Too still. Had he overstepped? Maybe he should've kept his hands to himself. Never his strong suit.

"Levi?"

"Yes?"

"That's one of the nicest things anyone has ever said to me."

"It's true." He was utterly crazy, but he needed to know if this was going to go anywhere. "Believe it." He cradled her face between both hands, his thumbs brushing her cheeks.

Her hands hung by her sides as though she didn't know what to do with them.

Levi slid his hands down and grasped hers, tugging her in. "Heather." He kept his voice quiet. Soft. Not only to keep Shelby from overhearing, but he didn't want to scare the woman in his arms, either.

She bit her lip. "Levi."

A thrill coursed through him at hearing his name spoken so softly. He pulled her a tiny bit closer and wrapped his hands around the small of her back. "Heather? May I kiss you?" There had been a time when he'd never have thought to ask. When it seemed his right to take. But those days were long gone.

Her gaze remained fixed on his, her eyes seemed to be trying to read into his soul. Then she raised herself on her tiptoes and leaned in with her lips parted slightly. Her eyes fluttered closed as she grasped his forearms.

That was a yes, right? Levi barely dared to breathe. He lowered his head to close the gap and brushed his lips against hers for one electrifying instant. Was that enough kiss?

Not nearly. His next attempt captured her lips. Tasted them. Caressed them. But he wouldn't push her any more than that. There was plenty of time. There was no need to rush anything, but her response was all he could've hoped for.

"Wow," she breathed, her eyes filled with wonder.

His sentiments exactly. "You know, this wasn't just a 'thank you' kiss for what you're doing for Shelby."

Her lips turned up at the ends a little, as though she found his words amusing.

Levi nuzzled the corners of her mouth lightly then tightened his hands around her back. "I wasn't looking for a girlfriend, but I might've changed my mind." He also hadn't been looking for a job in Helena, but he might've changed his mind about that, too.

Heather's gaze remained fixed on his, her pretty smile in place, but her eyebrows rose in question.

He was bungling this. "If you think you could handle being around me. I know this is a strange way to ask. To see if you might want to date me."

"I thought you'd never ask."

His heart thrilled. "I don't know what my future holds. Once Jared gets back, I don't have a job here anymore. I have one in Seattle..." At least, he hoped he did — a really good one. He allowed his voice to trail away, watching her for a response.

"I've only been in Helena for a year. I love it here, but there are many great places to live."

That was a good answer, right? It meant she was open to moving for him. But was he willing to stay for her? The siren call of the urban kitchen had dimmed.

"How did your day go with your parents on Thursday?"

Heather's eyes clouded as she looked away.

"Tell me," he whispered.

"My mom pointed out a zit on my face."

Levi's fingers drifted over Heather's forehead and cheeks. "I don't see a thing. Even if I did, it wouldn't change the essence of who you are."

"I covered it with makeup."

She'd done a remarkable job. Even at this close range, there were no hints. "Heather." He kissed her lightly. "You're beautiful. Don't listen to your mother. She's got her own set of problems, and she's taking them out on you."

She took a deep breath. "And my dad watched the football game, sat down briefly for dinner, then disappeared into his office."

Someday he'd meet her parents and set Mrs. Francis straight on a few things. Let her know it wasn't okay to talk down to Heather this way. And remind her father that his daughter needed him.

Levi had never known his own dad. Which of them had it worse? It didn't matter. It stopped right here. Jared was a terrific father. He could be Levi's role model. Or Todd, or Rob. Someday.

A flicker of light dawned in the back of Levi's mind. He had friends here now. For the first time in his life, he felt like he belonged somewhere. Was there really hope that he could start over? Find love? It was too strange to imagine, and yet there was a gorgeous, trusting woman in his arms.

Levi tightened his arms around her shoulders, letting his hands tangle in the blond hair that skimmed her shoulders. Heather nestled against his chest, and her arms wrapped around his waist. He was aware of every skin cell that pressed against her, but he'd be careful. She was worth it.

He stroked her shoulders, holding her close. "I want to find out — no, I need to find out — if you are something — someone — God brought into my life."

"I'd like to find out the same thing," she murmured against his chest.

CHAPTER 13

$\mathcal{H}$eather inhaled the scent of the Scotch pine in front of the bay window, so unlike the fake pre-lit trees her mom erected in nearly every room of their Missoula mansion, each decorated with a different theme. Just like she'd decorated a fake Heather for years.

This was more like it. A real tree, leaning a bit toward the window despite her and Levi's best attempts. Imperfectly draped with someone else's snowflake-shaped lights and decorated with someone else's baubles.

She lifted a photo ornament from the box. "Look at this! Shelby's first Christmas."

Levi's fingers brushed hers as he took it from her and turned it over.

Heather leaned closer and peered at the photo. "She was a cute baby, all pudgy with those pretty brown curls."

He glanced at her then took a step closer to the tree and slipped the ornament over a bough. "You want kids someday?" He turned toward the open box on the coffee table.

Heather's heart pounded at the offhand question. Her

answer mattered even though he feigned nonchalance. "Sure. Two or three, maybe. You?"

"I never really thought of myself as parent material."

She heard the rustle of packing peanuts as he sifted through them in search of more decorations. "If I were going by my parents, I wouldn't want to inflict that on my own children, either. But I'd like to think I can be a different kind of mom than mine is." She hesitated, but he didn't turn toward her. "You're good with Shelby. You'd be a much better dad than yours was."

"You can't know that."

Heather shot a quick plea for wisdom heavenward. "Just the fact you're aware of it proves my point. You're solid and grounded."

"Trying to be. Not always succeeding." He rounded the coffee table so it stood between them before facing her. His eyes held her captive, drawing her in. "Cooking is a demanding career. It doesn't leave much time for a family. Kids need a father who's actually around."

Although they could survive without one. Her dad hadn't paid her a lot of attention, but Levi didn't know his at all. Neither she nor Levi had thrived in those environments, though.

He was right. She'd always envisioned marrying a man with a nine-to-five. They'd go to their kids' soccer games and dance recitals, eat dinner together, and have weekends off to play and go to church together. That wasn't the sort of life Levi could offer her.

She bit her lip. He was worth it, wasn't he? And he might change his mind. He was still so vulnerable. His brother had overcome the past and was eager to add two needy little girls to their family. If Jared could do it, Levi could, too.

Besides... that kiss the other evening. She could only hope there'd be more tonight. Heather took a deep breath. "I think... maybe... it isn't something we'd need to decide right away."

Levi's green eyes darkened as he angled his head. "It's not a deal breaker? Because I can't promise to change my mind."

Heather rounded the coffee table and grasped his hands. "Not a deal breaker." She'd definitely pray about it, though. Seeing Bren's rounded belly had created a longing in her. As had Aimee and Jared's excitement to adopt from China. There was more than one way to create a family, but two people who loved each other could be a family without children.

Did she *love* Levi? She searched his face for clues as he tugged her closer and wrapped both arms around her, his hands splayed across her back.

"I don't deserve you, Heather." His lips brushed her jaw just below the ear with a tantalizing tingle.

She trembled from his touch. "I don't deserve you, either."

Did anyone deserve love? Deserve to find someone who took their upside-down life and flipped it right-side-up just by their very presence?

Her eyes closed and her knees weakened as he trailed whispering kisses along her jaw and down her throat. She clutched his face between her hands and captured his wandering mouth with her own. "Levi," she breathed.

This time he didn't hesitate. This time his kiss was sure.

Deep and demanding, the possessive stamp seared her soul. She was his. He was hers. No matter what happened in the future, she'd never be kissed like this again.

Heather's fingers tightened in the hair on the back of his head. He couldn't get away. He wouldn't. She wouldn't let him end this kiss now. Not ever.

He fell back against the sofa, taking her with him. She tumbled across his body and forgot the awkwardness soon enough as his mouth continued to possess hers, his hands slipping from her waist to her hips. Beyond.

A dim warning sounded in her brain at his urgent hands, but she silenced it in her need. Feelings she hadn't known existed swarmed her, stealing her breath, igniting a fire within her.

"Uncle Levi?" Shelby's questioning voice came from somewhere behind them.

The kiss broke abruptly. Levi pushed Heather away and surged to sitting. His gaze burned into her eyes as he fought for breath. Then he blinked and looked toward the staircase. "Yes?"

His voice was husky. If she spoke now, Heather's would sound similar, full of pent-up emotion.

"I-I just needed a drink of water."

Heather couldn't look at the little girl. What had she seen? How did the child's eight-year-old brain process the sight of her uncle and her caregiver locked in such a passionate embrace? Did Jared and Aimee ever make out like this in front of her? They wouldn't need to. They were married. They had a bedroom with a door.

What she and Levi had been doing passed those bounds.

"Go ahead and get one." Levi's voice still had a hitch to it.

"Okaaay."

Face flaming, Heather pulled further away from Levi and finger-combed her mussed-up hair. It was a good thing Shelby had come downstairs. What would have happened if she hadn't? "I, uh, need to use the restroom." And Heather fled.

LEVI CLOSED his eyes and dropped his head in his hands, listening to the soft footfalls of his niece as she crossed the tile floor to the kitchen, the clink of a glass, the water running from the faucet.

What had he been thinking?

Short answer: he hadn't been. He'd allowed passion to overcome his good sense and his hands to roam where they didn't belong. How could he have let himself? He respected Heather more than this.

She'd hate him. He deserved it. He hated himself. She was the best thing to ever happen to him, and he'd blown it all in one stupid moment. Or maybe it had been more like ten.

A gentle touch brushed his shoulder. "Uncle Levi?"

Did he have to face the little girl? "Yes, pumpkin?"

"I love you."

His heart twisted at the words. "I love you, too. Time for you to hop back in bed."

She kissed his hot cheek and darted up the stairs.

Levi crossed the space and splashed water on his face.

117

The other side of the kitchen island would be the safest place to be when Heather returned. She was sure taking her time, though. If the powder room had a window, he'd wonder if she'd pried it open and escaped.

Shelby's kiss and declaration of love were so sweet and innocent.

Did he love Heather? Or did he just want to have her? Big difference there. How could he even know, especially now? Things had been going so well, but this, this had bungled everything. So much for being a new man in Christ.

The powder room door whispered open, and Heather stood in the corridor in front of it, staring at him. Her face was pinker than usual — so was his, no doubt — and her eyes wider, as though assessing him.

"I'm sorry." The words blurted out of him. "I'm not sorry I kissed you, but it got out of hand. It's my fault. I shouldn't have." He braced his hands on the edge of the granite island.

"I think I should go now."

She probably should, but he didn't want her to. He wanted to make amends, to prove it didn't have to be this way.

Heather glanced toward the front door, as though determining whether she could escape before he caught her.

"Stay a bit longer? We haven't finished decorating the tree." And he was lucky the box of fragile ornaments hadn't hit the floor. They hadn't exactly been thinking about it.

She looked at the tree then bit her lip. "I'm not sure it's a good idea."

Levi held up both hands. "I promise to behave. I-I think we should talk."

"I'm not sure what there is to say."

He felt kind of the same way. Those kisses and touches had divulged far more than the English language had words for. More than they should have demonstrated. "Please."

Her arms crossed over her chest. "Despite what it seems like, Levi, I'm not actually that kind of woman."

"I know. And, believe it or not, I'm not that kind of man." Not anymore, at least. "I... it caught me by surprise, but it won't happen again. Not like that. I promise."

She swallowed hard. "I'm not experienced with this kind of thing. I've never..." Her hands did a little flap. "Never really... fallen in love before."

Love. Was it only lust he'd felt? No. Pretty sure not, but what happened to old things having passed away to make room for the new? But if he didn't explain to her now, when would it be easier? Maybe never, but once they'd regained their footing and she trusted him again would be a better time, right?

It had to be better later, because if he bared his soul tonight, she'd be gone for good. No more chances to redeem himself.

Imagining a life without Heather was suddenly impossible, whether he stayed in Helena or she moved to Seattle. He needed her like fish needed water and birds needed air.

"Have you... have you ever been in love?"

Golden opportunity, Esteban. Right here. Right now.

Instead, he shook his head. "I've never felt this way about anyone before." That part was certainly true enough, but was it love? The question burned in him. And if it was, could that be enough? Sure, the Bible said love covered a multitude of sins, but old Saint Peter couldn't have known

119

about Levi. About Heather. It was a generic saying. A platitude.

She came forward slowly until she stood opposite him at the island, her gaze searching his. "I'm sorry."

His heart thudded into the soles of his feet. He'd lost her anyway. He couldn't make it worse by telling her about his past. But how to start? He opened his mouth, moistened his lips.

"Levi, I need to go. I... I scared myself back there. I came on to you like a desperate woman, and now I don't know what I feel. My emotions are still surging every which way, and I don't trust myself. I don't want to ruin what we've got. If it isn't too late."

"You haven't ruined anything. It's all me. I'm the one who started it. I'm the one who should have kept in better control. I'm the one who should be sorry, not you. And I am." The urge to go around the island and take her in his arms nearly overwhelmed him. That would be so much the wrong thing to do. The wrong way to prove his words. "I'm sorry, Heather. Can you forgive me?"

Those troubled blue eyes gazed back at him. "It wasn't just you."

She was right about that. Once the initial shock was over, she'd given as good as she'd received, but that didn't change the facts. "Please forgive me." Would it help if he knelt on the floor? No. She'd think he was proposing or something.

Proposing? His brain was still going too many directions at once. She was right. They needed a bit of space.

"I forgive you, Levi. If you can forgive me. We crossed a

line tonight — maybe not that far, but still, too far. It can't happen again. From either of us."

"I forgive you. And I promise it won't happen again."

"Good night. I'll see myself out. And we need to pray." She crossed to the foyer and slid her feet into her tall boots before reaching for her warm coat.

Pray.

Levi stood rooted to his spot behind the island. Even a sweet goodnight kiss was a bad idea after all that. He watched as she left the house, lifting his hand in response to her slight wave.

An icy wind blasted in while the door was open. A chiller he should have felt half an hour ago. He rested his elbows on the island and massaged his forehead, trying not to remember the electrifying touch of her hands.

Lord? What do I do now? I think I might love Heather. I don't even know for sure. She says she forgives me, but time will tell if I wrecked everything by losing control. Can You fix this mess?

Of course God could fix it. The bigger question was, would He?

CHAPTER 14

So, how was Nicaragua?" Heather had avoided the resort dining hall as much as she could the past few days. It went right along with Levi texting her to send Shelby downstairs when he got off work. Anything to keep out of his path... or the path of a friend who might be too perceptive.

But she couldn't slam her apartment door on Marisa's face.

"Pretty good." Sauntering into the suite, her friend raised her eyebrows at Heather. "But, didn't I tell you about it last weekend?"

Oh. Right.

"Haven't seen you around much this week, so I thought I'd pop in and see what's up. How're things with Mr. Hunky Chef?"

"Uh... can I fix you a cup of tea?"

Marisa chuckled. "Only if you give me the scoop."

Heather turned toward the tiny kitchenette. "Not really anything to talk about," she tossed over her shoulder.

"Ha. I don't believe that for a minute."

Had God sent Marisa in answer to Heather's prayers? Who else was there to talk to, to trust, to offer counsel? Five days hadn't cleared her mind. Not at all. She busied herself with her back to her friend. "Can I ask you a question?"

"Sure. Go for it."

"You and Jase were engaged for over a year. How did you — you know — manage? I mean, physically." Or maybe they hadn't, and now Heather had put her friend on the spot. Oh, man.

Silence stretched.

"Never mind. It's none of my business. Would you prefer green tea or chamomile?"

"Green tea would be great. As to your question, I'll answer it on one condition. That you tell me why you asked."

Tears stung her eyes. "It's okay."

"Heather."

"Um-hmm?" Still no eye contact.

"That kind of question doesn't come out of a vacuum."

Too true. She'd given away more than she'd intended to. Both the other night to Levi, and now, verbally, to Marisa. She took a deep breath and let it out slowly, turning to face her friend. "Okay."

"It was a tough year. I'll be honest. I did a lot of traveling across the US as Miss Snowflake. Jase accompanied me a few times, early on, but that was difficult. No accountability, if you know what I mean. So we decided it was best if he remained in Helena, where he was acting as general contractor for building our house. Plus, he had photography shoots. When I was home, I stayed out at the farm with Bren. You might recall she took over the CSA operation in February that year when my mom remarried and moved over to Bob's place."

Heather nodded. "That was before my time, but I remember hearing about it. And then when Bren married Rob, they bought the farm from your mom, right?"

"Right. But back to the question. Jase and I made two conscious decisions. One, that we'd never be alone in a secluded place where we couldn't easily be interrupted. And two, that we'd read the Bible and pray together to end every date. That really helped keep us grounded in remembering to do things God's way."

Two really good decisions. Ones she and Levi had not made. But hadn't Marisa admitted the decisions came after finding the difficulties of keeping their relationship pure? Maybe it wasn't too late for her and Levi, either.

"I won't lie," Marisa went on. "It was sometimes hard to remember that even if we slipped up and no one found out, God would still know. We really wanted to present our marriage to Him as pure. I had to force myself to stop fantasizing about what would come after the wedding. It would have been easy to jump the gun."

Heather fixed the two cups of tea and handed one to Marisa. Was it her turn to speak now? She didn't want to. Really, really didn't want to.

"Tell me about you and Levi."

"We didn't have sex. But we came a bit too close, and now we don't know what to say to each other." Scratch that. All Heather could think of to do was evade the man completely. Wouldn't that night have been the perfect time for him to tell her he loved her, if it were true? Sure, they'd only known each other a month, but they'd seen each other every day. Spent many hours together.

Who was she kidding? A month was way too soon to declare love.

But it didn't seem too soon. She'd fallen for Levi Esteban hook, line, and sinker. And that had resulted in giving him more than she'd meant to.

"So you don't trust yourself now."

Marisa's quiet words wormed into Heather's mind, and she nodded. "I don't fully trust him, but it's me I really don't trust. I never expected to feel so... so overwhelmed."

"Do you love him?"

"I-I don't know. I've never been in love before, and I'm confused." She'd said those words to Levi. Been vulnerable to him even in that, but it had seemed like he'd held back in his response. Maybe she was just a Christmas fling to him. A man who couldn't live life without a woman at his side, even temporarily.

No. Not the Levi she knew. He wasn't like that.

"It's hard, isn't it? Falling in love is like a dance where you both have two left feet. It's almost impossible to navigate without either party feeling pain a few times. We're two people getting to know each other, unintentionally stomping on each other's vulnerable spots. How can it be all sunshine and roses?"

"I guess that makes sense." Heather clutched her teacup. "But when you've kind of gone too far, how do you get back on track?"

"It takes time. And prayer."

"I'm praying, and I'm sure he is, too. But we don't have a

lot of time. Aimee and Jared expect to be home right before Christmas, and then Levi's headed back to Seattle. That's only three weeks away."

Marisa quirked a grin. "It's not like Seattle is on a different planet. Sure, it's a solid day's drive, but it's not impossible."

"I suppose." It seemed like it, though. Heather met her friend's gaze. "What should I do now?" Because wait and pray didn't seem like much of an answer.

"Bro. Ask her already." Jared's voice came through the laptop speakers. "The tickets are bought and paid for. Consider it our Christmas gift to you."

Aimee's voice murmured something in the distance.

Jared chuckled. "Never mind. Aimee says we have a different present for you. But either way, we can't get a refund on the tickets, so please use them. And don't take Shelby, either. I bet she could stay at Rob and Bren's that night, if you ask."

"But she's my responsibility."

"She has sleepovers at her friends' houses. It's fine to ask. Or Todd and Kristen's, but I think they're planning to go to the concert. You and Heather should go with them."

Levi sighed. "I think she'll turn me down."

"You haven't talked in a week? Then it's time to step up your game, bro. She's really nice. Aimee approves."

"You seem to forget that I won't have a job in Helena when you return from China. It's better to just let this drift away." Everything in Levi cried out not to let go, but logic still paralyzed him.

"There are other good restaurants in the city. Have you dropped off résumés? There's Lucca's Italian, for instance. Or you could try the Silver Star."

None of them was the Fireweed. And, if Levi were being honest, none of them was the Grizzly Gulch, either. "I don't think my future is in Helena."

"Aw, I'm sorry to hear that. Me'n Aimee hoped you'd stick around and be a hands-on uncle to the girls. All of them."

Shelby was definitely growing on him, and Skyping with Mei and Yun had endeared the two little ones to him as well. Still, Levi shrugged. "A man needs a job. You know that."

"Promise me you'll look for something there?"

"No promises, but I'll think about it."

"And pray."

"Yeah. Learning more about doing that, too. Still can't quite figure out why God cares about every little thing, though."

"Because He loves you even more than your big brother does."

That got a chuckle out of Levi. "I guess."

"So are you going to ask Heather to Christmas at the Cathedral? It's Sunday evening, and you're not working. Turn on the Esteban charm."

His gut soured. He'd already turned on too much of it. Not something he was willing to discuss with Jared via Skype. If at all. Ever. "The Esteban charm isn't all about letting one's big brother pay for your dates."

Jared rolled his eyes. "Quit making excuses. You've fallen for Heather Francis, and now you're letting her go for some reason you haven't quite explained." He waited, staring into the webcam for a long moment before shaking his head. "Don't give up without a fight."

If only that didn't mean what he thought it did. Trying to pick things back up with Heather meant talking about what happened between them and coming clean about his past. Sure, she knew he'd grown up rough and become a Christian in just the past few years. Maybe she'd assume that he hadn't exactly lived a moral life, but what if her mind hadn't gone there? If he were really going to pursue her, he'd have to tell her.

That's why he stayed away, hoping for the Second Coming of Christ so he wouldn't have to deal with it. Or he'd settle for a meteor. Anything, really, to keep from having to see more hurt and disappointment in Heather's blue eyes.

Anything... including letting her go?

"Gotta go, bro. Let me know what she says." Jared's face disappeared from the screen.

Levi logged out and closed the laptop before going up the stairs and into his brother's bedroom. Tucked into the mirror frame lay two concert tickets. He pulled them out, read them over, and stared into the mirror. What did God see in him?

As far as the east is from the west, so far has he removed our transgressions from us.

Psalms said God forgave him and sent his sins packing. But Heather wasn't God. Levi tapped the tickets against his palm. What did he have to lose? If he didn't fight for her, he'd lose her anyway. Right. The difference was she'd know his secrets.

But he'd asked her to forgive him already. Asked God, as well, and God had set him free. Who had tightened the bars on his cage? Had he done it to himself?

Levi tugged his cell phone out of his pocket and tapped the photo of Heather he'd taken that day long ago. His heart thundered in his ears so he wasn't sure he'd even hear if she answered.

"Hi, Levi." She sounded breathless.

"Hi. I, uh, I was wondering if you'd like to go to Christmas at the Cathedral with me on Sunday evening. I'd really like to take you." Suddenly, it was true.

"I've heard it will be an amazing performance of Handel's Messiah, and the Cathedral of Saint Helena is stunning."

"That's what I hear, too. And, besides, we wouldn't want Jared and Aimee's tickets to go to waste. I mean, I'd like to go with you, anyway."

"I'd like to, but only on one condition."

Levi's heart sank. Always with the bargaining. "What's that?"

"That we talk. Really talk."

"You mean, about... what happened the other day?" Because, no, he wasn't ready. He'd never be ready.

"Yes."

His thoughts battled within, swinging sharp swords and taking his voice as prisoner.

"Never mind then." Disappointment welled in her words.

"No, wait." When he was sure she hadn't hung up, he

kept going. "We can talk. Maybe after the concert?" Because if they talked before, she'd probably call off their date and he'd have to explain to Jared why the tickets sat unused. And, because he wanted just one perfect evening to remember her by.

"Okay. If you're sure."

He let himself exhale. "How about we go for dinner beforehand? I hear Lucca's is good." And expensive, but Heather was worth it.

"If you wanted, we could double with Marisa and Jase? They're going to Lucca's before the symphony. I wonder if their seats in the cathedral are near ours?"

Levi hoped not, but doubling for dinner might be a good idea, if for no other reason than it would keep the conversation from veering places he wasn't ready to face.

CHAPTER 15

*H*eather had never stepped foot in Lucca's before. It just wasn't the kind of restaurant a woman went with her girlfriends. She gripped her satin clutch as Jase opened the door and swept his hand to indicate everyone should precede him. Marisa entered first, looking right at home in the upscale setting.

Levi's hand rested on the small of Heather's back as she followed. She could feel the warmth of his touch through her winter coat, or maybe it was just her acute awareness of him.

The creamy yellow walls glowed, mottled by the cylindrical pendant lights and wall sconces. Dark wooden beams high on the wall displayed wine bottles, while lower down, local artwork created focal points.

"We have a reservation," said Marisa. "Mackie for four."

"Of course. Right this way." The maître d' led them to a square table in the corner.

Levi pulled a wooden lattice-work chair for Heather and seated her across from Marisa before taking his own seat.

Her eyes caught on his and held for a long moment. That green. Sure, Jase's eyes were somewhat green as well beneath his red hair, but not the startling shade of Levi's, set off by his thick dark hair.

A rustle across the table caught Heather's attention. She glanced up to see Marisa's smirk. Heather's face heated. But was it so bad to find the man she was dating attractive? *The man she was dating.* Were they really? Would they find their way through this swamp of their own creation to find solid ground in their relationship? Tonight was a test.

Jase opened his menu. "Anyone for wine?"

"Not for me." Levi shook his head then glanced at Heather. "Go ahead if you like, but I drank too much for a few years, and it's best I stay clear of alcohol."

The least she could do was support him in that. "None for me, either."

"No problem. We'll pass as well. The food is amazing." He grinned at Marisa. "Remember the first time we came here?"

The look Marisa returned to her husband was full of gentleness and adoration. "Just before Christmas at the Cathedral two years ago. Our first date after we got back together."

Heather looked between them. That was a story she wanted to hear another time. She stilled her heart as she took in the list of entrées and the prices beside them. Whoa. She'd better not get used to this.

"You should find out if they're hiring a chef." Jase looked across at Levi. "I don't imagine they have a lot of staff turnover, but you never know."

"Great idea." Marisa's hand pressed over Levi's for an instant. "We'd sure like it if you stayed in Helena."

Levi gave a nervous-sounding chuckle. "Right. Because an Italian restaurant wants a Mexican chef."

"Don't knock it." Jase grinned. "It was started by a British guy. And besides, the US is multi-cultural, right down to the dining. You don't need Italian genetics to cook Italian cuisine."

"I don't know. I'm expecting a promotion when I return to Seattle. The Fireweed is opening a new location in spring, and I'm in line for that."

"Yeah, but is it as posh as this?"

Heather held her breath as Levi took a moment to look around. Then he nodded. "I'd say the Fireweed is a couple of steps beyond this. Very urban and left coast."

It probably had prices to match then. Not that Heather hadn't tasted and enjoyed the meals Levi had created at the Grizzly Gulch. She just hadn't realized how far his world was from hers. Not just Seattle to Helena, but the Fireweed to... to Taco del Sol or the Parrot Confectionary.

She didn't fit into Levi's world. She should've known that. For all he wore cowboy garb often when off duty, he craved city life and filet mignon. Well, she'd settle in and enjoy the whole experience tonight. The fine Italian dining and the magical Christmas at the Cathedral. After that was soon enough to come back to earth.

They ordered appetizers and then pasta while carrying on a light conversation. Heather had never imagined lasagna made with Italian sausage and mushrooms, but it teased her taste buds and melted in her mouth. So, so good.

"How are things gearing up for the Miss Snowflake

pageant?" asked Jase, looking between her and Marisa. "Only a week to go now."

"Everything's in place. The contestants' rooms are prepped downstairs at the Tomah House, and everyone has received her agenda."

"And I have a list of places to be with my camera." Jase chuckled as he reached for his glass of water, clinking with ice cubes. "Good thing the younger girls don't have a full week of activities slated out. The Christmas Eve finale is enough for them. Charlotte visited us a few days ago, and she's practically ricocheting off the walls in her excitement. She figures she'll win this year."

Heather smiled. "She might. But don't rule out any of the Little Misses." She glanced at Levi. "Shelby has been working very hard, too. I think she fancies taking the crown."

He scrunched his face to one side.

Seriously, a guy who couldn't wait to return to his upscale Seattle life still turned his nose up at the pageant? He didn't even make sense.

"Well there's more to life than a tiara." Marisa giggled. "And many things are better than a crown."

Tiaras and crowns were forever out of Heather's reach now. She was done competing for fleeting recognition. Done succumbing to her mother's begging. Marisa was right. Life was meant to be lived and, while winning would be nice, it wasn't her essence.

"Oh, I meant to tell you," Marisa went on. "Just to keep you up to date. One of our judges canceled due to her son being in a motorbike accident. She thinks he'll pull through, but feels her place is at his side right now."

"That's totally understandable." Thankfully the judges' side of things wasn't Heather's responsibility. "Is Kristen looking for someone else, or are we running with four?"

"Four isn't ideal in case of a tie." Marisa bit her lip. "Kristen's on it. It looks like Tahira Aquino might be able to fit it in. Have you heard of her?"

Heather felt the blood drain from her face. "Tahira?" She managed to keep her voice even. "Isn't she the star of that new soap opera? She's been in a few movies."

"Yes, that's her. She has a background in pageantry. In fact, that's how the Hollywood talent scouts found her to start with."

That entire fateful evening flooded into Heather's mind. "In Los Angeles ten years ago. I remember." All too well.

Marisa angled her head. "Were you in that competition?"

Suddenly the last few bites of the lasagna held little appeal. "I was actually in the lead through most of it. That last night there was a protest as we were entering the venue. An egg smashed on my face then I tripped and got an elbow to the eye." Heather shook her head. "I've always been such a klutz. Getting pushed around in that crowd threw me off my game, I guess. I really blew that last evening and wound up as second runner-up. Tahira won."

"Oh, I'm so sorry. We can look for someone else."

"No, it's okay. It's not Tahira's fault that whole thing happened. She won fair and square. She probably won't even remember me."

IT'S NOT Tahira's fault that whole thing happened. It's not Tahira's fault that whole thing happened.

Heather's words replayed in Levi's mind over and over, louder than the symphony lifting off the roof of the Cathedral of Saint Helena, louder than the soaring mezzo soprano. They looped right alongside his memories of that night, the jostling crowd. He'd been there. Part of the problem.

Oh, Heather was right, to a point. Tahira'd had nothing to do with the protest, but the organizers of it had meant for her to win. Levi hadn't been a ringleader, just part of a minority crowd in college, eager to take offense.

A blue-eyed blonde had been in the lead, and his friends hadn't been able to handle the thought. They'd drank a bit too much and gone down to the convention center to even things out.

The blue-eyed blonde had been Heather.

He'd helped ruin her chance to win and break up that streak. Twenty-seven losses. Even with her mother pushing her, that showed amazing perseverance.

Levi didn't want to think about Tahira Aquino. More had happened later that night. Much more. But how could he protest the Snowflake pageant's choice of judges? Besides, Tahira wouldn't likely remember him the way he remembered her. She wouldn't expect to find him here. He was only the chef, and she'd gone on to Hollywood fame and stardom. He could stay out of the judges' way. The resort was fully booked for competition week. They'd never have to run into each other.

He'd make sure of that.

Beside him, Heather leaned slightly forward, her lips

slightly parted as her eyes focused on the soloist. She was so pure. She didn't deserve Levi.

The words of the chorus filtered in.

Let us break their bonds asunder, and cast away their yokes from us.

He needed the bonds of his past broken. Desperately. He'd been staggering under the load way too long, trying to make a fresh start, but look at last week. Given a bit of temptation, the old Levi was in control. Could God really give him complete healing? How did that even work? Wouldn't his past always be his past?

Yet... did it have to affect his future?

Levi squeezed his eyes shut, but that only brought Tahira's beautiful Afro-Asian face to mind with her glowing brown skin and sparkling eyes.

He was stuck with his past.

Hallelujah! for the Lord God Omnipotent reigneth. The Kingdom of this world is become the Kingdom of our Lord, and of His Christ: and He shall reign for ever and ever.

The chorus exulted as they sang how Jesus came to wipe it all away. Levi's heart lifted with the crescendo.

King of kings, Lord of lords.

It was easy to get caught up in day-to-day life and forget what was really important. Levi bowed there in the Cathedral of Saint Helena and allowed the words of the centuries' old musical, laden with scripture, to roll over his soul.

I know that my redeemer liveth, and that He shall stand...

Yes. The Christmas season was here to remind him of the tiny baby that had come to redeem the world. To redeem *him*. To make him new. God in flesh.

Worthy is the Lamb that was slain, and hath redeemed us to

God by His blood, to receive power, and riches, and wisdom, and strength, and honor, and glory, and blessing. Blessing and honor, glory and power to be unto Him that sitteth upon the throne and unto the Lamb, for ever and ever. Amen.

Levi's own problems were minuscule in comparison to the victory and majesty of God's descent to this planet. He reached for the peace offered by the final victorious chorus.

Silence descended on the cathedral when the final notes drifted away. He could barely breathe. Could barely remember anything but the spiritual encounter.

It took several minutes for the first attendees to gather their coats and slip out the side door in silence. A few rows ahead of them, Jase's arm tightened around Marisa's shoulder as she leaned against him.

Levi couldn't do that with Heather. Didn't dare after what had happened. Not knowing what would happen in the next week or two. Would he return to Seattle and try to forget Heather? He wouldn't be able to. She'd stamped his very soul.

Before he could even dream of a future with her, he needed to tell her at least the generalities of the life he'd lived before Christ. She needed to know, and he'd promised. She didn't need the specifics, though. Didn't need to know about Tahira.

His conscience bit.

But where did he draw the line? He'd repented before God and been forgiven. Was there any need to delve into that night in L.A.?

Heather's fingers tightened around his, and he stared down at their entwined hands.

God? I need Your guidance, because I sure can't figure this out myself.

"Wasn't that incredible?" Heather whispered. "Thanks for asking me, and please tell Aimee and Jared thank you, too."

"It was amazing." And so much more. Levi took a deep breath. "I'm glad we came."

CHAPTER 16

*D*id you Skype with your mom and dad this morning?" Heather glanced in the rearview mirror of her car.

Shelby nodded, her lower lip trembling. "I miss them. Why can't they be home now?"

"It will be worth it. They'll be here in a few days with your new sisters." She'd had a quick Skype session with Aimee herself.

The little girl looked out the window at the passing snow-covered city. Everyone had begun to worry whether they'd have a white Christmas this year or not. To say nothing of a sledding party being a tad difficult without snow. It had come, though, fast and furious, over a foot in just a couple of days. And the party was on, just like that.

"I don't want new sisters. I just want my mom and dad."

"Oh, sweetie. Remember how excited you were? You'll be such a great big sister. Mei and Yun need you."

"I don't need them. I don't want to share. I told Mommy to leave them in Beijing."

Uh oh. "What did she say?"

"She said she couldn't. They're already Estebans and they're leaving soon. It's too late to give them back to the orphanage." A tear slid down the little girl's quivering jaw.

"Well, that's great they're coming soon, right? It takes a long time to travel from China, but they'll be here before Christmas." Early afternoon on the twenty-second, from what Aimee said. Not much time to spare if flights were overbooked or something else happened to detain them, but it was the best they could do.

Out of city limits now, the highway out to Hiller Farm stretched in front of the car, and Heather applied her foot to the accelerator. The tires slipped a little in the snow, but held when she eased back. She glanced in the mirror again. "Today will go quickly, because you'll have a good time with your friends. And Uncle Levi will be coming to the party in just a couple of hours when he gets off work. I bet he'll build a snowman with you or take you down the hill."

Shelby's lip quivered as she nodded.

The child had done so well up until this last week. Now it seemed her world had turned upside down, and she couldn't stop missing her parents. What did Heather know of that? Even though her mom and dad hadn't paid her much attention, at least they'd been present. Aimee and Jared would make up for it. Shelby didn't need to worry.

Maybe she was feeding off Levi's mood because, for goodness sake, the man had been twitchy all week. Not only had he not lived up to his agreement to tell Heather what was going on in his head, but he was back to avoiding her. How was he going to spill his secrets when he avoided being alone with her? The staying in public was probably a good idea after that evening on the sofa, but couldn't they find a compromise somewhere? He was busy working with Opal and Axel to prep all the meals for a full house for the week, being as Jared wasn't home yet. And, after work, Levi was devoted to Shelby.

As it should be.

Probably.

Frustrated, Heather turned into the drive at Hiller Farm, where the parking area near the greenhouses had been plowed and liberally sanded. Already kids whooped with glee as they careened down the hill on crazy carpets, donuts, and sleds. Davy Santoro, Lila's older brother, was hard at work with his buddies building a large barricade of snow along the country road, with another being erected about twenty feet away. There'd be some epic snowball fights coming soon.

She turned off the car. "There's Charlotte and Lila, having hot chocolate with Mr. and Mrs. Delaney. Want some? We can stop by the bonfire first."

"I guess."

Hopefully, Shelby would snap out of it soon, before Levi arrived. Or before Dr. and Mrs. Mackie began to question if Heather was doing a good job as a caregiver. Now that her foot was finally healed, she was back to maintenance part time, but only while Shelby was in school.

"Shelby!" squealed Charlotte. "I thought you'd never come."

With a backward glance, Shelby allowed her friends to tow her away. Heather released a sigh and made her way to the bonfire.

"Can I pour you a cup of cocoa, hon?" asked Marisa's mom.

Heather pushed out a smile. "Thanks, Wendy. I'd love one."

"I'll get it." Wendy's husband, Bob, ladled steaming hot chocolate into a mug from the big pot over the camp stove. He grinned at her. "You look in need of a few marshmallows."

"I won't say no."

He added a generous scoop and handed it over. "Here you go. How's that foot doing?"

Heather cradled the mug close, allowing the steam and rich, chocolatey aroma to bathe her face. "It's fine now. Thanks for asking." Although she'd rather everyone had forgotten. That hadn't been her finest moment. What *was* her finest moment? She didn't have one. And where had that thought even come from?

Bob peered past her. "So where's your young man?"

Good thing she hadn't taken a sip yet, or she'd have spewed it everywhere. "I don't have a young man." Only in her dreams.

Wendy chuckled. "Marisa told us you and Levi went for dinner and to the symphony with them last weekend, and we'd heard other rumors, too."

"Oh." If those passionate kisses had meant anything — hopefully there were no rumors attached to *them* — she'd been on the verge of having a boyfriend. But then, well... who knew? Heather forced a laugh and shrugged slightly. "We've gone out a few times, but it's nothing serious. He's headed back to his job in Seattle after Christmas."

Please, Lord, not before they'd really talked. For

Heather to tell him what he meant to her, which was a whole lot more than the physical attraction they'd shared. She loved him. And he'd break her heart by leaving.

Bob hitched his pants as he eyed her. "Seattle's a nice place," he offered. "As cities go."

Not that Levi had invited her to join him. It sounded like his life there was full. Full of work, like Dad, who never seemed to stop thinking about investing, or checking up-to-the-minute stock reports. Was Levi like that? Always testing out new recipes, looking for new suppliers, focused on nothing but his restaurant?

There was no room for Heather in a life like that. Dad had pushed her to the side in favor of work all her life. He'd said, somewhat indulgently, that it was to pay for all those pageants her mom entered her in. To give her a life of plenty. But all she'd wanted was his love. His time and attention.

It seemed so clear now. Just like with Dad, she was second best with Levi. His work came first, and it likely always would. How could she have set her heart on a man just like her father?

Heather blinked back the moisture in her eyes. "Like I said, it hasn't been anything serious. Certainly nothing to give up my life here for. Someday my prince will come." She gave Wendy and Bob what she hoped was a dazzling smile and turned away, eyes searching for Shelby.

There she was in that pink snowsuit, spinning down the hill with Lila. The sound of both girls' squeals pierced the air.

Thinking about following Levi to Seattle was stupid, but maybe her time in Helena was over, too. Maybe she was done with every aspect of pageantry. Maybe clumsy people like her shouldn't work in maintenance, either. Maybe it was time to put her financial degree to work. Could she do that and not become like her father? Would working in his field be a way to regain Dad's favor? As if she'd ever had it to start with.

THE PARKING AREA at Hiller Farm was jam-packed when Levi arrived, the entire place a hive of activity. He parked along the road and got out of his car to survey the scene, inhaling the crisp air. In Seattle, it was probably gray and rainy. Here the sky was bright blue with a few fluffy white clouds.

Several adults appeared to be in a rough-and-tumble face-washing fight with a pile of squealing, rosy-cheeked kids in damp snowsuits. Looked like the younger generation was winning. More children slung snowballs from behind icy barricades while an army of sagging snowmen looked on, occasionally getting in the crossfire. Farther back on the property, kids screamed as they soared down the hill on an assortment of saucers and sleds.

He picked Heather out by her bright blue jacket, climbing up the hill with Shelby's pink snowsuit beside her. The other two were likely Charlotte and Lila. He owed a lot to Heather for all the good care she'd taken of Shelby. She'd offered to bring his niece out to the party, but there she was, actually participating instead of sitting around with the adults.

Not that a lot of adults seemed to be bystanders. He

made his way along the greenhouses to the bonfire.

"Welcome, Chef Levi!" Bob Delaney rose from his lawn chair and shook Levi's hand. "Can I get you a mug of cocoa? We've got some Christmas cookies, too." The man grinned. "Even you can't make better ones than my Wendy. We've got mocha peppermint pretzels and cinnamon swirls and gingerbread angels."

Levi smiled at Marisa's stepdad. "Sounds good." He accepted the cocoa and a cinnamon cookie then motioned toward the hill with his chin. "Good turnout."

"It's our fifth annual." Wendy nodded with a smug smile. "Thankfully people bring treats to share, because the event has grown so much we never know how many will come."

"It's just an open house?" Levi didn't know of anyone else who'd do that. Even the Mackies charged for events like the Halloween party. Though, come to think of it, that had required a whole lot more coordination. All this party really needed was snow and a place to warm up from it.

"It started when Marisa and I joined the Tomah CSA with the farm, and she began inviting single moms on social assistance to garden here with us." Wendy pointed out the area closest to the road where snowballs zinged across a battlefield. "Soon we had half a dozen young families growing food and learning to cook and can." Her eyes misted over.

"You done real good with that." Bob squeezed her hand. "You and Marisa."

Wendy blinked. "Bren is our biggest success story. She took over the management two years ago, and then she and Rob bought the farm from us after they were married last spring. It seems natural to keep having the sledding party here. Bob's place doesn't have a good hill like this one." She glanced over to where Bren and Rob sat on the front deck of the farmhouse. "This has been a hard pregnancy for Bren, so I worried it would be too much for her. But she was okay with us just taking over and doing it like we've always done."

Levi tried to think when he'd last done something big, something magnanimous, for others. Just because he wanted to make them smile. Covering Jared's shifts in the resort kitchen and watching Shelby didn't count. The Mackies were paying him a good wage, and he'd needed a break from Seattle, anyway. Watching Ellison Benoit bungle around the Fireweed's kitchen had reminded Levi he hadn't taken a vacation for three years. Good timing to draw from that fund.

Was he ready to go back? Helena was great, but he couldn't see himself cooking at a place like Lucca's. The food had been excellent, but there'd be no room for his own creativity with an Italian menu set in stone. He needed the Fireweed, where the executive chef could flex with the seasons and whatever was available.

He'd had some of that freedom at Grizzly Gulch, too. Opal might be the boss, but she didn't micromanage the other shifts as much as most head chefs he'd worked under.

Levi's gaze found Heather on a toboggan with three little girls, skimming down the hill and catching air on a bump. All four of them spilled off into the soft snow, their giggles carrying across the crisp air.

He couldn't help grinning, but the smile disappeared as quickly as the cinnamon cookie. He needed to talk to Heather. Today. Now.

CHAPTER 17

*H*eather had never felt more aware of her flushed cheeks and mussed-up hair, at least if she wasn't thinking about that evening a few weeks ago. Which she wasn't. At all.

She stared up at Levi at his question. "Go for a walk?" Man, she even sounded dazed.

"Please?" His green eyes looked at her solemnly, and no smile poked at his cheeks. "Kristen said she'd keep an eye out for Shelby for a bit."

This was The Talk, then. Suddenly, she didn't want to hear whatever he had to say. No matter if she'd made it the stipulation for last weekend's date. They'd had a great dinner, but Levi had seemed awfully quiet, at least toward the end of it, and he'd barely said anything at all after Handel's Messiah. Not that she'd felt talkative, either. She'd wanted to savor the beauty, the majesty of the experience.

But now.

"Okay." She owed it to him, after all. They'd clear the air. He was leaving the resort soon, and so was she, not that she'd told anyone yet. But she would. The restlessness inside her demanded a change. If it couldn't be Levi, then something else.

They wandered along the plowed country road, shoulders bumping occasionally. For a guy who wanted to talk, he sure wasn't doing it.

Finally he cleared his throat. "I'm really sorry about what happened a couple of weeks ago. About how I, I took advantage of you."

Hadn't he already apologized? Like five times? "It was both of us. I'm sorry, too." That evening had ruined a promising relationship.

"The thing is, that was the old Levi. The kid who was shuffled around in foster care, who ran with the wild ones, who didn't know Jesus. The new Levi... well, there's no excuse."

She couldn't think of a thing to say, so she nodded and picked up her pace.

"Back then, when I was a teen and in college, I did whatever I wanted. It was all about the moment. About what would feel good right then."

Was he saying what she thought he was saying?

"I didn't care about consequences. About hurting people. It was all about me."

Just spit it out, buddy.

"You asked if I'd ever felt this way before." He inhaled sharply. "Physically, yes. I'm not proud to tell you that. I couldn't tell you how many times. How many women."

Even though she'd suspected as much, his admission cut her to the core.

"Emotionally, no. I've never cared about anyone before,

Heather. You, you're different. You're worth so much more than a scumbag like me could ever offer. I haven't had sex with anyone since I became a Christian four years ago. Haven't really wanted to until, well, two weeks ago. I forgot myself. Forgot Christ redeemed me."

Could she live with that? How much did his past matter? He was a believer now, and on a new path. And he was totally not the only one to blame for that evening on the sofa. She could have stopped him — stopped herself — much sooner. She hadn't. She'd lost herself to his touch as much as he had to hers.

"So, that's what I needed to tell you." He hesitated. "There's more, but that's the gist of it. I get that you'll hate me, but you probably do, anyway."

She touched his arm and turned toward him. "Levi?"

His fists clenched at his sides as he stared into her eyes.

"I forgive you. How can I hold your past against you? Like you said, you were a mixed-up, unloved kid, and you didn't know any better. Everything is different now."

Levi's jaw twitched and he looked away.

She had to make him understand. "I'm just as much at fault."

He shook his head, not meeting her gaze.

Why couldn't he see it had been both of them? Hadn't he felt her hands on him? He definitely had.

"I appreciate that you forgive me, Heather. It means... it means a lot to me."

Should she take a chance? What did she have to lose? "I told you I'd never fallen in love before, but I have now." That was as close to saying the words as she could get past the lump in her throat.

Those green eyes flicked to hers and then away. He stuffed his hands in his pockets.

Heather's heart froze solid. She'd handed the opportunity to him, a gift on a platter, a crown at the end of a competition, and he rejected it. By his silence, he rejected *her*. She was still a loser, only now she could add loser in love to her list of dismal accomplishments.

She spun around on the slippery road. "Never mind." Her footsteps took her back toward the farm, where she could still hear squeals and laughter in the distance.

"Heather, wait." His hand caught her sleeve, halting her.

She stared down at his long fingers then shook them off. "I said, never mind. I get that you can't wait to leave Helena. You might say you care about me, but I get that I'm not enough for you. So, fine. That's how it is."

"It's not how I want it to be."

Heather glared up at him. "It's in your court, buddy. You have the power to change those things. You have the ability to accept forgiveness, mine and God's. You have the ability to love someone. You don't have to be so blasted stubborn."

"Heather."

"What? If you've got more to say, then get it out already. I'm done with your games. Either you hate me or you love me. We're not *just friends*, and we can't ever be. Not after what we shared. What we did to each other. So what's it going to be?"

Man, what was with her mouth, giving him an ultimatum like this? But he'd been hot and cold for almost two months now, and she was done. She knew her feelings, and she knew his. If he wouldn't acknowledge them, where did that leave her?

Dismissed.

"Shelby's all yours for a ride home." Heather jerked away from Levi and strode down the road. Back to her car, where she buckled in, jammed her key in the ignition, and drove away.

WHETHER SHELBY'S on-and-off tears for the past four hours were due to missing her parents, too much activity, or her uncle's curtness with her, Levi had no idea. But finally she was in bed and, if the silence didn't lie, asleep.

Leaving Levi with nothing but his thoughts.

Why couldn't he have said the words Heather had desperately wanted to hear this afternoon? He would've gotten them out if it hadn't been for Tahira Aquino showing up Monday afternoon for the pageant festivities.

It wasn't only random faceless women he'd slept with. One was Tahira. On the night Heather had lost her best bid for a crown.

His fault. All his fault. He'd tried to confess even that, but the words just wouldn't come out. He was already way beneath Heather's upscale privileged upbringing. Scum to her purity.

If only he'd never realized the triangular connection, but he had.

He found himself in the kitchen, pulling out baking chocolate, eggs, butter — his way to soothe his mind. He'd promised brownies to Heather, but that was a bad idea. Better to let the break be clean.

As though it could be. She'd strode down that snow-covered road, the bright sunshine gleaming off her royal-blue jacket, jumped straight in her car, and drove out like a boss.

The break had started two weeks back, and jagged shards had lined the path ever since. Nothing clean about any of it. He felt the searing wounds deep in his heart. Everywhere he looked around Grizzly Gulch Resort — even here in his brother's house — he could see her laughing, talking, smiling at him. If that sofa belonged to him, he'd drag it to the dump. All he could see, hear, and feel, was Heather pressed against him. It was a memory that needed to disappear. Once he'd have drowned himself in alcohol to obliterate it, but Tahira proved drink wasn't a permanent solution. He wasn't going down that road again.

He whipped that butter within an inch of its life then focused on melting the chocolate without scorching it.

Like it mattered. Who was going to eat this, anyway? He sure didn't want to, and there was only so much a weepy eight-year-old could handle. Shelby. She'd spend the next two days with Heather now that it was Christmas break from school and her parents weren't back yet. All that around the stupid pageant starting tomorrow afternoon. Heather was going to be doubly busy, but she hadn't complained. It seemed she was as attached to Shelby as his niece was to her.

Gah.

He cracked eggs into the mixing bowl then started on chopping walnuts. If he kept this up, he'd make powder out of them.

With the pan finally in the oven and the scrubbed mixing bowls tipped upside down in the drain rack, Levi pulled out his laptop at the kitchen island. The sofa would've been more comfortable, but he was avoiding it like the plague.

An email from Gisele at the Fireweed popped up in his queue. His finger trembled as he tapped to open it.

Dear Levi,

This letter is to inform you that we have offered Ellison Benoit the position of executive chef for the new location of the Fireweed, and he has accepted.

We trust your extended leave has been restful and that you'll be ready to return as sous chef at the current location on January second.

Please advise me by return email.

Sincerely,

Gisele LeBlanc

Levi slowly exhaled as he read the brief words over again.

He hadn't nailed the promotion. His creativity would still be guided by someone else. By the owners' nephew, even though Levi had been at the Fireweed longer and had more over-all experience. Guess that's what he got for not being related... and probably for taking leave this fall. It likely hadn't helped him any. It had just been excruciating watching them dote on Benoit, and Jared's request had come at his breaking point, the perfect excuse to get away for a short time.

He'd hankered for a fresh start designing menus at the new upscale location within walking distance of Safeco Field and Benaroya Hall. Gisele had scored a premium site, and he should be the executive chef bringing it to potential.

But they'd given it to Benoit. To an upstart with half the experience. Half the talent.

Keep his old job… or walk away?

What choice did he have? No one else was offering him a living wage after Christmas Day. There was no job in Helena that enticed him. Just a woman.

Levi shook his head.

A woman that wasn't for him. That he'd have to keep a secret from forever, and he wouldn't be able to do it. It was no way to start a marriage.

Whoa.

He sat back against the stool. Marriage? Who was hearing wedding bells?

He could see Heather floating toward him down the aisle of New Song Fellowship in a shimmering white gown, a jeweled crown holding her veil in place. Love shining from her blue eyes just for him. Giving herself to him in the way God intended. He could envision his niece as flower girl, a reception catered by his brother out at the resort, a honeymoon in Hawaii…

Snap out of it, Esteban.

Only a dream. Dreams didn't come true. Not for guys like him, who held secrets that could never be revealed.

He dumped the steaming brownies in the trash.

CHAPTER 18

*W*hat a day, with the formal gown competition still to come. The main floor of the historic Tomah House housed twenty-two women for the remainder of the week, each hopeful to be crowned Miss Snowflake on Christmas Eve.

Heather felt old, even though a contestant or two had her beat in years. All these poised, glamorous women had visited the Capitol today for a photo op with the Mayor of Helena, the Governor of Montana, and assorted other dignitaries, most of whom would be present for the pageant events.

She had a closet full of gowns herself from the past few seasons, and couldn't bother trying to justify spending more when this was the last pageant she'd ever conduct. No one cared what the director looked like. Her job was to organize the ready room, offer last minute advice, and keep things humming in the background.

That lavender dress would do tonight. She had a different one for every evening this week. Then she'd donate them all to charity. They'd hardly be fitting for a female investor. Business suits were in her future, not that she'd told Dad she was finally going to take him up on his offer.

Avoid Tahira Aquino. You only need to survive this one week. That's all.

The mantra worked just fine until she slipped into her seat at the banquet a couple of hours later. What on earth had Kristen done, seating her at the same table as the actress? Like they *wanted* to catch up, for old times' sake? Not hardly. But she couldn't make a fuss.

"Heather? Heather Francis?"

Her worst fears realized. Okay, that was too dramatic. Her worst fear had been Levi Esteban walking away, and it had already happened. Heather had nothing left to lose.

"Yes, that's me." She'd love to pretend she didn't know who the elegant Afro-Asian was, but that wasn't going to fly. "Good to see you again." Social lying wasn't really a sin, was it?

"I thought I recognized you. You're just as lovely now as you were a decade ago."

And just as uncrowned.

Heather smiled. "I've been following your career. You must be very pleased at the success you've found in Hollywood."

Tahira's dark eyes lit up. "I can't believe it's legal to have so much fun every day and make so much money doing it."

Oh, she was good. "It only happens for a lucky few, I guess." Heather picked up her soup spoon. Would she be able to get even a dribble of this consommé down her clenched throat?

"I know. I'm still so amazed I got this chance. I grew up dirt poor in an immigrant family in Los Angeles, but on the other side of the tracks from Beverly Hills where I live now, if you know what I mean."

Heather knew what she meant. Doubtless everyone at the table knew.

"That pageant was everything I'd ever dreamed of. I'd grown up watching Crowns for Kids on TV and then Miss America. All the pageants, really. I couldn't believe when the Filipino community offered to sponsor *me*." Tahira's hand, glittering with half a dozen jeweled rings, rested on her chest.

If all this was supposed to make Heather happy for the other woman's win, it was failing. Not that she'd always given a lot of thought to the other contestants' backgrounds or the reasons they entered. Pageantry didn't encourage thoughts of anyone but self. Did that make her egocentric?

"Wow, I'm sure it was exciting for you." *Lame response, Heather.*

"I know, right?" Tahira sighed dramatically. "And then I was approached by a talent scout... and then those commercials... and then I landed supporting roles in all those movies." She shook her head with a giggle. "And now to be the lead on Love and Lawyers with all those hunky stars ostensibly fighting over me, it's just too much."

The consommé was too much, too. Heather laid her spoon down. Why wasn't anyone else at the table talking? She glanced around and met Priscilla Abercrombie's eager eyes.

Oh, great. The only way this evening could be worse was

if Levi was at the table, witnessing her nose being rubbed in her biggest defeat.

"It's such a pleasure to meet you, Ms. Aquino." Priscilla leaned over the table. "I wasn't aware you know our Ms. Francis."

Heather managed not to snort.

"Oh, we competed in the same pageant a while back. Was it ten years, Heather? I'm afraid I've lost track."

"About that." Would this evening never end? How many courses did this dinner have, anyway? Manny removed her soup bowl and replaced it with an entrée. Slices of lamb and chunks of roasted potatoes sent alluring aromas upward. Too bad she wasn't hungry.

She glanced at Priscilla's plate, where rings of acorn squash, stuffed with quinoa and mushrooms, held center stage. Guess she was still vegetarian. Maybe it hadn't been a show at Halloween after all.

Heather had tried to avoid Levi back then, too. He'd been so rude about the pageant. No surprise he wasn't anywhere in the dining hall tonight. Yes, she'd had a good look around while she stood at the ready room door. He'd have had to get a sitter for Shelby, of course. Children weren't invited until Christmas Eve, when they had their own pageants to compete in.

"Oh, I had no idea," gushed Priscilla. "This is so exciting. How fabulous for you to have such a wonderful friend."

Was she talking to Tahira or to Heather? This evening kept getting better and better.

"You never told me you were friends with someone so *famous*."

Friends was totally the wrong word.

Heather cast a helpless glance at the other five diners at their table. Three were having a quiet conversation between themselves. Two looked to be enjoying the sumptuous meal. The only escape was... well, escaping, and as the pageant coordinator, she couldn't very well do that.

"Heather's never won a pageant," Priscilla informed Tahira in a confiding tone. "She does her best to teach our children poise, but it's not really the same as if she'd worn a crown herself."

"Oh?" Tahira's gaze landed back on Heather.

On the other hand, maybe excusing herself from the table wasn't such a bad idea, after all.

"CHEF LEVI? HAVE A SEAT."

"Yes, sir." Levi settled into the chrome and white leather chair opposite Dr. Mackie. Once this sterile office had reminded him of home. Now it jolted him with its minimalist design, so out of place amid the rustic style of the rest of the resort. If he focused on that, maybe he wouldn't feel his burbling gut. Surely this was simply a parting interview.

"You've done well for us, son." The older man's eyes assessed him from across the glass and steel desk. "You once mentioned you'd like a letter of recommendation when your term here was over. I'd be happy to write one for you. I know an innovative chef of your caliber will go far."

Levi swallowed the lump in his throat. Should he accept the letter, the praise? Because the position he'd wanted most had already gone to someone else. He didn't need a recommendation to keep his old job, and there'd be little room for creativity. Ellison Benoit had gained that privilege. Still, he had to say something. "Thank you."

Dr. Mackie grinned even as his head shook. "Sure wish we could keep you."

"I know you can't. With Jared back, you've got a full staff." Levi had borrowed the resort van to pick Jared's family up from the airport a couple of hours ago. Shelby needed her parents' arms around her as desperately as the culture-shocked tots did. It was going to take a while for the household to find its new balance.

"Right. He'll be putting in morning shifts through the holidays. Would you be willing to work twelve-to-eight for the rest of the week? I hate to switch things up on you, but Opal could use an experienced hand with all the pageantry dinners. They're really not her thing."

It would give him an excuse to stay until after Christmas rather than return to his empty Seattle apartment. Its great view of Puget Sound didn't make up for the silence. Still, he'd enjoyed it before and he'd enjoy it again... after a family-style Christmas where he'd be careful not to start anything back up with Heather that he couldn't finish.

"Yes, Dr. Mackie. I can do that." He rose. "If that's everything, I'll check in with Opal now."

At the resort owner's nod, Levi exited the office and glanced over the log rail into the lobby below. His feet welded to the commercial carpet as his ears started ringing.

How could he get past Heather and Tahira chatting in the middle of the lobby? Sure, there was an emergency exit from the mezzanine, but sounding the security alarm would draw even more attention. Could he stay up here until they left the space? But Opal expected him in the kitchen. Was there any chance they wouldn't see him? What was he worried about, anyway? Heather wasn't speaking to him — he'd made sure of that — and Tahira wouldn't recognize him. One weekend ten years ago. He'd changed a lot since then, right?

It had to be enough, because otherwise he was trapped for who knew how long, and he was on duty. Levi pulled out his phone and pretended to study it as he trod lightly down the stairs. Just a few yards across the corner of the lobby and he could dive into the dining room and enter the kitchen from that angle.

"Levi?"

Doom settled its icy fingers around his heart. Could he pretend not to hear Heather's voice? No. It hadn't been all that quiet.

Still, what were the odds of Tahira recognizing him? Slim to none. He glanced up just enough to acknowledge Heather. "Hi, there. Sorry, I'm busy."

"You look like death warmed over."

She'd stopped him to tell him *that*? Seriously?

"Uh, I'm fine. Opal needs me in the kitchen. Gotta go."

"I just wanted to sa—"

"Levi? Is that you? Levi Esteban?"

If he'd thought the world stopped minutes ago, now it was spinning backwards. Ten years of rewinding zipped by in a flash. He couldn't do it. He plowed into the dining hall, rounded the corner, and leaned against the wall, heaving.

Be sure your sins will find you out.

But he'd repented! Asked forgiveness. God had wiped

his slate clean four years ago. He was a new man in Jesus. Except for the way he'd handled Heather that evening.

How could God still love him? How could God forgive him... again? For not treating the woman he loved — yes, loved — as the crowning glory she was.

Voices from the lobby caught at him.

"Yes, Levi Esteban. Do you know him?"

Tahira chuckled, that low seductive laugh that no doubt had clinched her soap opera stardom. "I sure did, once. He's a hot lover boy and, oh, my. Those emerald eyes. I've never seen anything like them."

"His eyes are unique." Heather's voice. Emotionless.

"We met after that protest in L.A.. You remember the one. Those blazing eyes locked onto mine from the midst of the crushing crowd, and I knew I had to find him again afterward. If you know what I mean."

Levi slid down the wall until his butt hit the floor. He cradled his head against his knees. *Lord, please. Please. Please.*

"Oh, really."

"I asked the protest leader after the pageant — oh, trust me, I didn't have anything to do with that little demonstration! — and she knew who I was talking about. I mean, those eyes, right? She got us together. One of the best weekends of my life."

"Well, he hasn't changed much. You're welcome to him."

A moment later Levi heard the lobby's automatic doors swish open and shut. He pushed himself to his feet and, steadying himself against the wall, made his way into the kitchen.

There was pretty much no way his life could get worse.

"re you in here, girl?" Marisa's voice came through the wood paneled door at the Tomah House as she knocked.

Heather coughed and hoped it sounded convincing. "Not feeling well," she choked out. As if that weren't the understatement of the decade.

"I'm coming in and making you tea."

"No, it's oka—"

The door swung open.

A person couldn't tell Marisa what to do. Heather sniffed. No doubt she looked as dreadful as she felt. Her hair was a mess, her face hot and blotchy from crying, and the pile of sodden tissues on the coffee table should tell the rest of the story. "Just leave me alone."

"Nope. I'm not worried about catching what you've got."

How could she know? Heather turned and blew her nose.

"So, a cup of tea. Tell me what happened." Marisa swept into the kitchenette.

"Nothing to tell. I don't feel well."

"And I'm the Queen of Sheba."

At least she'd been queen of something. Unlike Heather, who was a loser through and through. She couldn't even fall in love with a decent guy. Hot lover boy indeed.

The kettle clanked as it hit the burner. "About Tahira Aquino."

"I don't want to talk about her."

"You've heard, then."

Oh, she'd heard, all right.

"She's telling everyone she spent a weekend with Levi way back when. Right after a pageant she won. Which, if memory serves me, is a pageant you were competing in. Leading in."

Tell me something I don't know. Actually, please don't.

"He said he'd been roped into demonstrating against the dominance of white girls in pageantry."

Of course. That made so much sense. Not that it made a difference. Her heart was already at rock bottom. Heather glanced up in time to see Marisa's eyes roll.

"Which is dumb, if you ask me. I've met plenty a contestant and winner from assorted ethnic backgrounds. At any rate, it was years ago, before he became a Christian. If that's what's bugging you, I think you need to forgive him. He's not that guy anymore."

The kettle whistled, and Marisa turned back to make tea.

Heather sank onto the sofa and dabbed her eyes with a clean tissue. "That's not true," she blurted.

"What's not true?"

"He's still the same. I told you."

Marisa set two cups of tea on the coffee table, nudging aside a pile of tissues. "You told me, but let me repeat. He's not that guy."

"You didn't see where his hands were." Or where Heather's had been. Her cheeks burned at the memory.

"There's a big difference."

Heather stared at her friend from bleary eyes. "Oh?"

"With you, he stopped. He apologized."

They'd only broken apart because Shelby had caught them. Would he have stopped if his niece hadn't come in? Would Heather? Ah, that was the real question, wasn't it?

"Look, I'm not whitewashing what you guys did. You went too far." Marisa held up both hands. "And no, I don't want to know the details. But here's the thing. Even if you'd gone all the way, that's still not something God can't or won't forgive. It's still not something you couldn't forgive each other for. Levi's a believer, Heather. So are you. So you messed up. We all sin. What you did isn't any worse than pride or jealousy. Don't you get it? Jesus covered it all with His death on the cross. Not just the stuff you did before you were saved, but the stuff you've done since then. Everything."

The battle raged inside Heather. While the words felt true — *were* true — how could she possibly grasp them?

Marisa took a sip of tea. "We missed a few Sundays when we were in Nicaragua, so I've been catching up with Pastor Grunewald's sermons. You know which one I just listened to? The one where he talked about the church being God's crown. Remember that one?"

Memories flooded back. For a brief moment she'd clung to being God's delight, His crown of joy. After church, she'd gone to the mall with Levi and Shelby. She'd felt like she'd been offered a fresh new start.

"Read Isaiah sixty-two, Heather." Marisa pulled her cellphone out of her hip pocket and poked around for a few seconds before handing it over. "Here. I'll wait."

Why did Heather have such bossy friends? But she needed them. Needed them to point her back to the Lord. She accepted the phone and began to read.

Jerusalem... You will be the crowning glory of the Eternal's power, a royal crown cradled in His palm and held aloft by your God for all to see.

People won't talk about you anymore using words like 'forsaken' or 'empty.' Instead, you will be called 'My delight' and the land around you 'Married,' because the Eternal is pleased with you and has bound Himself to your land.

Be called married? Heather glanced over at Marisa, but her friend's eyes were closed. Praying, no doubt. She read on.

As a young man marries the woman he loves, so your sons will marry you, Jerusalem. As a groom takes joy in his bride, so your God will take joy in you.

Heather blotted her eyes with another tissue and scanned down the chapter.

So ready yourselves to pass through the gates, from old to new. Clear the way for the people; make it clear, easy, and straight. Unfurl the banners that proclaim these people are renewed!

Say to the daughter of Zion, "See, your salvation is coming; your liberation is on the way — God's reward is with Him: His work is by His side."

And they will be called 'The Holy People, Redeemed by the Eternal;' Jerusalem's new name will be 'Desirable City, No Longer Forsaken.'

"But that's Jerusalem." It sounded too good to be true, but that's because it was. She wasn't the capital city of God's precious nation.

"Pastor Grunewald explained, remember? Paul echoes many of the same sentiments in his letters to the churches, so I don't think taking it personally is too out of context."

Heather wasn't a church, either. She was just a woman, unloved, uncrowned, unwanted.

"By the time Isaiah was a prophet, the nation of Israel had been whoring after false gods for centuries. They'd cycled through more seasons of rebellion and repentance than anyone can count. And still God loved them. You've got nothing on Israel, sweetie, and we're talking about the same patient, loving God."

Was it that simple?

So ready yourself to pass through the gates, from old to new. Clear the way for Heather; make it clear, easy, and straight. Unfurl the banners that proclaim Heather is renewed!

Tears dribbled down her face. No longer tears of self-pity, but tears of acceptance. Of reaching for her identity in Jesus. It wasn't found in pageantry. Oh, she'd known that all along, but this time, it felt clearer.

LEVI LOWERED himself onto the sofa at his brother's house. Good thing that piece of furniture wasn't telling any tales, not that it would matter with the gossip Tahira had smeared across the resort in just a few short hours. Now everyone knew what he was really like.

Shelby clambered up on his lap while his two new nieces stood hand-in-hand at the foot of the stairs, staring at him with wide dark eyes. A cleft palate looked no better up close than it had on the screen. He smiled at the two youngsters, and they backed up a step.

Apparently he was terrifying. What else was new?

"Uncle Levi, Mommy says you're going back to Seattle soon."

He kissed Shelby's forehead. "In a few days."

"I don't want you to go. I'll miss you."

"I'll miss you, too, pumpkin."

"Then stay."

"I can't. I have a job there." Even if it wasn't the one he wanted.

Jared scooped up the two smaller girls and settled into the easy chair across from Levi. "Have you looked for something here? Because Shelby's right. We all want you to stay."

"I doubt if the Mackies do. Not anymore." Levi raised his eyebrows at his brother. "I'm sure they've heard the tales. I know you have."

Jared shrugged, and Mei snuggled against his chest. "It's ancient history, bro. Water under the bridge. She can't make it into anything more without your help."

"Right. But that's not all. I'm just not sure with Heather..."

Shelby tilted her head and looked up at him.

"What about her? Sounded like you two were an item there for a bit?"

"Can't talk about it right now." Levi tousled Shelby's hair and looked pointedly at his brother.

"Hey, Shelby, someone gave us a big box of clothes for your sisters. Why don't you go upstairs and help Mommy sort through it?"

"Okay." She bounced away and scrambled up the stairs. At least someone seemed to have regained her equilibrium.

"So, what's up?" asked Jared when a door closed upstairs.

"It's more than Tahira. Heather knows I cost her the crown in L.A.. Knowing what I did with Tahira afterward only grinds her face in it that much more."

"How did you cost her the crown?"

Wasn't it obvious? "She was in the lead. Getting jostled in the crowd knocked her off her focus, and she lost. Tahira won."

"Might that have happened even if you were holed up in your apartment studying?"

Like a college kid should've been the weekend before finals. Instead, he'd blown that off, too, flunking out and drifting from one menial job to the next for several years before Jared sponsored him for culinary school. He shrugged.

"Levi. It's not your fault. You didn't make the decision. You weren't a judge. Yeah, you shouldn't have been there, taking part, but you didn't tip the scale."

"You're right. I guess."

"You confessed your sins and gave your life to Jesus. Bro, He's forgiven you. You don't need to wallow in the past. Sit down with Heather and explain it to her."

"She... she kind of hated me before she found out about the pageant. About Tahira."

"Do you love her?"

Levi nodded slowly. "Yeah. I do, but she doesn't love me back." Although she'd said she did, out at the farm, and he hadn't responded when he had the chance. His pride had caused him to choke. It was too late now. Wasn't it? He shook his head. "It's really complicated."

"Will you regret leaving her without clearing the air? Because you're not the first couple on the planet to have a fight. To misunderstand each other." Jared cradled his two Chinese daughters in his arms and pressed a kiss onto one mop of shiny black hair, then the other. "Love isn't easy, bro, but it's totally worth fighting for."

"But my job..."

"You said Benoit got the promotion."

"But I still have a job. It's still the Fireweed." Still one of the top restaurants in Seattle, but how long would that last with a rookie at the helm? Yet what else could Levi do?

Jared leaned forward. "Open a restaurant here."

"No." Levi shook his head. "I don't have that kind of money, and where would I find investors? Besides, I wouldn't want to pull business away from the resort. The Mackies are good people, and you've built a great menu here."

"Opal's been the driving force of that, which I've come to peace with. Cooking day shift allows me more time with Aimee and Shelby, and now the little ones. My identity doesn't come from my job. Not anymore."

Levi wanted what his brother had. Oh, not Aimee, but that kind of relationship. Where his job was just a job, but his life was wrapped up in a loving home with Heather and a crew of little Estebans at his side. Kids with blond hair like hers, dark hair like his, or even different colored skin.

He wanted it with all his heart. Was there any way to make it come true?

CHAPTER 20

*H*eather's car was packed. No one needed to know it contained pretty much everything she owned, other than the pile of formal gowns on the bed with a note to donate them. She'd email an official resignation to Dr. Mackie right after Christmas, but she just couldn't stay at Grizzly Gulch Resort without Levi. Or with him.

It was time to grow up. Time to make use of her college degree, which had nothing to do with pageantry, building houses, or taking care of children.

Finance.

She was oddly a little excited. Maybe she and Dad would find something to talk about to make up for the silence sure to come on the heels of Mom's shock. He'd always said he'd make room for her at the office and teach her the ropes of investing. She could only hope he meant it.

Heather adjusted the drape of her single-shoulder gown and examined herself in the full-length mirror. Her makeup covered every flaw, every trace of every tear she'd shed over the past several days. She'd pulled her blond hair into a bun low at her nape, held in place with sapphire-tipped pins that matched her dangly earrings.

Chin up. This was her last pageant. She'd go out at the top of her game. From here on out, it was crisp white blouses paired with black pencil skirts and tailored jackets. She could rock those.

She took a deep breath and pushed her feet into snow boots then wrapped herself in a silvery shawl and picked up her matching heels. Kristen had already texted from her car in the parking lot. They both needed to be at the Civic Center well in advance of tonight's final, ready for the contestants as they arrived.

"Nervous?" asked Kristen as Heather slid into the leather interior.

"Yes."

Kristen chuckled and put the car in gear. "So's Charlotte. She's been talking smack all week about how she'll win but, when Auntie Marisa came over to help her get ready, she was shaking."

The sound of a ringing phone came through the car speakers, and Kristen glanced at the display. "Rob? Just a sec, I need to get this." She tapped a button on the dash.

"Kristen? Can I drop the kids off at your house? Bren's gone into labor — really fast, really hard — and I don't think we can make the banquet. I need to get her up to the hospital. It's so early."

Heather's heart stilled.

Kristen tapped the brakes. "I'm on my way to the Civic Center. Is Lila ready? If she is, you can bring her and Davy to meet me there. Or I can send Todd out to pick them up."

Muffled voices for a few seconds, as though Rob covered the mouthpiece. "She's not ready. She says she doesn't want to go."

"Rob? It's Heather. I'm in the car with Kristen. I can help Lila finish getting ready if you like, but do you know something? If she doesn't want to participate, she doesn't have to. It doesn't matter that her name is in the program. There's a whole lot more to life than pageantry." Something she was finally figuring out herself.

Kristen glanced across the car in the light of a street-lamp. "Heather's right. The kids are welcome to come either way. They can sit with Todd and Liam. We'll take care of them. That's what friends are for."

Relief sounded in Rob's voice. "You sure? I don't want to push Lila."

"Absolutely sure."

"I'll throw in the bag with her dress, just in case she changes her mind. It's ready to go anyway."

"Sure. Sounds good." Heather let out a breath. "We'll all be praying for you and Bren."

"Now get going, Rob!" Kristen chuckled as she tapped to dissolve the connection. She glanced at Heather. "That sounded like the voice of experience speaking."

"It was. No kid should be forced."

But how was Heather going to leave this group of people behind? Friends who were there for each other? Who worshiped together, worked together, played together? How could she trade that in for a power suit?

But it was time. She'd make new friends. She'd have to, or her life would be far too empty.

HIS LAST DUTIES for the Grizzly Gulch Resort, and he was back in the cramped Civic Center catering kitchen. He, Axel, and Opal had prepped all week even while managing a formal dinner every night of the pageant. Jared had resumed the morning shift.

"Good evening, ladies and gentleman. My name is Dr. Mackie, and I'm your host tonight. It is my privilege to welcome you to the final evening of the third annual Miss Snowflake Pageant."

The voice through the speaker system was Levi's cue. He signaled Manny, whose tribe of black-garbed waiters picked up platters where slivers of golden roasted beets nestled in endive leaves amid mushroom tartlets. The waiters ghosted silently amid the white-clothed tables, setting down their burdens.

"We'll start out this evening with the pageant for girls ages seven through ten. Eleven young ladies have prepared to entertain you this evening. Please give a big hand to our Little Misses!"

Applause resounded through the ballroom.

"Go ahead, Levi." Opal made a shooing motion with her hands. "I know you want to see how your niece does."

He didn't need a second invitation, but pressed his back to the wall beside the kitchen door as Dr. Mackie introduced them, one at a time. Shelby was fifth. She paused, beaming for Jase's camera, then mounted the steps to the platform to take her place beside Charlotte.

Girls of various heights, of various shades of hair and skin, all linked arms and performed a line dance together. Emily Abercrombie giggled, and the emotion rippled through the line.

Levi couldn't help grinning at the infectious sound. A bunch of kids having fun together. Learning some manners, some poise, some public speaking skills. They weren't dolled up into something fake or divided by race. He'd been wrong.

Across the ballroom, Heather stood in a pose similar to his beside the ready room door. His breath caught at the sight of her in that glamorous dress. Her eyes would pop with that color of blue. How he missed seeing them up close.

The line of girls streamed toward her, and, smiling, she bent to greet them as they exited the ballroom. Dr. Mackie took the mic and soon the strains of *Joy to the World*, sung by hundreds of voices, filled the air. Soon the children were back on stage to perform their talents. Shelby wobbled in landing her string of cartwheels. Lila refused to sing. Charlotte's fingers tripped at least twice in her piano piece, not that Levi was an expert.

A little girl with chocolate skin performed a mime routine that had the audience chuckling. Levi would put his money on that one.

Meanwhile, the waiters brought back empty platters and made the rounds again with bowls of roasted butternut soup. He really should be in the kitchen helping, but maybe he'd done his share?

At last, the girls returned in their pretty dresses and lined up for the question segment. Dr. Mackie made a show of drawing a name from one bowl and a question from another to demonstrate impartiality.

"Miss Shelby Esteban, here is your question." He unfolded a paper. "If you could change anything in the world, what would it be?"

Shelby's hands trembled as she accepted the mic and looked out at the audience.

Levi held his breath.

"I'd want no one to have a cleft palate, and if I couldn't change that, I'd change how people look at them. Because they can't help it, and they're real people, like my little sister Yun."

The audience applauded, but none louder than Levi. Good for Shelby. She'd come a long way, even in the past few days.

After Sanura Thomas had been named Little Miss Snowflake and all the girls had sat down with their parents, Levi turned back to the kitchen. He didn't much care who won the other categories, and he'd left Opal and Axel to carry the load long enough.

He'd catch Heather afterward, when they were both off-duty. It was time they had a heart-to-heart.

THE EVENING DRAGGED, but Heather kept the smile pinned to her face until all the younger contestants had joined their parents around the tables. None of the girls in her deportment classes had won. Not the Little Misses. Not the Junior Misses. Good thing her decision to set pageantry behind her was already made.

She glanced across the ballroom to the table where Dr. Mackie sat, front and center, with his elegant wife on one side and Tahira Aquino on the other. The other four judges sat at the flanking tables, all of them making notes as the women's competition got underway.

Heather opened her phone and glanced through the email she'd already prepared. She might as well send it now. It wasn't like Dr. Mackie would be checking his phone at this stage of the evening.

Tap.

There. Sent.

"Goodbye, Levi," she whispered, as she gathered her things and stepped out into blowing snow. Time to call a taxi to take her back to Tomah House. Wouldn't her parents be surprised to see her so late on Christmas Eve?

"BEFORE I PRESENT Miss Snowflake to you, I have one announcement to make." Dr. Mackie's voice came through the speakers, and Levi paused to listen, as did the other kitchen staff.

"Many of you know Bren and Rob Santoro. It's my privilege to announce the birth of their son, Oliver Salvador Santoro, about half an hour ago. The only other detail I have is that mother and baby are doing well. Hopefully that goes for the father, as well."

The audience laughed and cheered.

Levi could only hope someone had told Lila and Davy

ahead of the public. Heather would be excited about the baby. She wanted a house full of kids. So did he.

"Okay, that's everything," said Opal. "Levi, you're free to go. Axel, you have the final cleanup under control?"

"Yes, ma'am." Axel grinned and saluted.

Levi made his way around the outskirts of the ballroom as Miss Snowflake was crowned. He didn't see Heather anywhere in the crowd — that blue dress would stand out — so she must have returned to the ready room. He tapped lightly on the door and poked his head around. The lights were off. Flipping the switch revealed an empty room. No coat. No boots. No purse.

His gut sank. He pulled out his phone and tapped her pretty picture. It went to voicemail after only one ring. He wasn't leaving a message. He needed to talk to her. Like, in person.

Back out in the ballroom, he caught Kristen's gaze where she sat at a table with her parents. She excused herself and glided toward him.

"Where's Heather?" he whispered.

Kristen grimaced. "Dad got an email from her about half an hour ago. He kept checking it hoping to hear from Rob. Otherwise it would have been turned off."

Levi latched onto the one word. He didn't care about the rest. "An email?" Dread swarmed his guts.

"She gave her notice, effective immediately."

He grabbed at the doorjamb to keep upright. "She what?"

"You heard me."

"She's not here."

"But she rode over with me. She didn't have her car."

"Doesn't change that she's left the building." Half an hour ago? How far would she be? Maybe he could catch her yet. "I'm going after her."

Kristen's hand rested on his arm. "Let me know."

He gave a curt nod then pulled his keys out of his pocket.

Minutes later he pulled into the main parking lot at Grizzly Gulch Resort, but the place she usually parked her car was empty. She hadn't been gone long, though, by the bare gravel rectangle when the rest of the lot was covered with an inch or two of snow.

He tapped her icon again. Still no answer. "Heather, it's me. Levi. Where are you? We need to talk."

Levi willed his phone to ring, but it didn't.

Where would she go? *Think, Levi. Think.*

He bounded up the stairs to her room on the second floor of Tomah House and knocked. No answer. He tested the knob, and it turned easily in his hand. The place was empty except for a mound of ball gowns on the bed. He picked up the paper on top. Donate them all to charity?

Buzzing circled his senses. She'd planned this.

While he'd been slowly coming to his senses amid a crazy busy week, she'd planned this.

He'd never told her he loved her. This wasn't how he wanted to do it, but it was all he had. He tapped her icon one more time and waited for the beep.

"Heather, I guess you don't want to talk to me, and I can hardly blame you, but there's something I need to tell you. I love you. I hope you hear how much I mean that. I love you. I want to tell you every day. I want to show you. Please, Heather. I love you more than life itself. I love you more than Seattle. I love you more than cooking." He forced a laugh. "I love you more than chocolate brownies. I love your laugh. I love the way your eyes sparkle. I love your heart for kids. I love that you love Jesus." How long could he talk before the voicemail cut out? Would she even listen, or just delete it straight up? "Heather, please call me. I can't live without you."

CHAPTER 21

*H*eather?" Mom stood silhouetted in the doorway, her pink chenille robe wrapped around her. "We weren't expecting you until morning."

"I didn't see any need to stay for the entire evening, once my charges were through the pageant. So I decided to come tonight. Merry Christmas!"

"Well, you're welcome, of course." Mom stepped aside. "Charles! Look who's here."

Dad appeared in his office doorway, his white button-up open at the neck and his cuffs rolled up twice. His casual look. "Hi, Heather."

Heather quailed. This was the life she wanted for herself? Surely she could work with numbers and not become addicted like Dad. It had to be possible. Besides, it was time to set aside her mother's way and embrace her father's. Time to grow past the glitz and glitter that had never loved her in return.

"Well, do come in. You're letting in the entire snowstorm."

187

"Sorry." Heather entered as her mother retreated. No hugs. No kisses. No warm welcome from either of them. Had she expected any different?

"Let me take your coat. Then tell me, how did your girls do?"

Moment of truth. "None of mine were winners."

"Oh." Her parents exchanged a look.

Might as well get it over with. "I made a decision. I'm done with it all. Dad, if your offer still stands, I'd like to put my finance degree to use."

Mom's hands fluttered. "Now, don't be hasty. There's a lot—"

"Are you serious?" Eyebrows raised, Dad straightened.

"Of course she's not serious. She's just had a bad run. Everything will be fine. I heard about a competition in New York I think you should enter, darling. I was going to forward the link to you."

"No. I'm not doing it. Never again."

"But, Heather, it sounds—"

She shook her head. Whatever it took to make her mother understand. "No."

"But—"

Dad's eyes bored into her. "Let the girl speak for herself."

Twenty-six, and still 'the girl?'

"It's over, Mom. I tried to make you proud my entire life, and I've never succeeded."

"We're proud of you. Aren't we, Charles?" Mom's gaze flitted between them.

"Of course. You're our daughter."

Heather's phone rang. What was that, the eighth time

since she'd left Helena? She hadn't answered once, and she wasn't starting now. Whether it was Levi, or Kristen, or Dr. Mackie didn't matter.

"Aren't you going to answer that?" Mom demanded.

"No."

"But it's ringing. Someone is trying to reach you."

Uh. Yeah? "You're the one who taught me not to let gadgets interfere with face-to-face conversations."

Her parents exchanged another look. "You haven't taken off your coat yet. Do come in. Your father can get your overnight bag."

Wait until they realized she had everything she owned in that car. "It's okay. I'm dressed for it. I'll get it. Be right back." Heather fled down the sidewalk. Coming home was a bad idea. She wanted — needed — a do-over, but how was this helpful?

Her phone chimed. Another voicemail. Maybe Bren had had her baby. Heather wanted to know that, right? She thumbed on her phone. Missed call and voicemail from Levi. A whole column of them. This was an awful lot from a guy who wielded the silent treatment like a weapon. Had something happened?

Her finger poised on the voicemail icon. She shook her head. Far too much had happened, and Tahira Aquino was the crowning touch. No, Heather wouldn't give in. She was going to get herself straightened out before she let another man anywhere near her heart. Spend a year or two focused on becoming a successful businesswoman. Yes. That.

It sounded dreary. Lonely.

Why was Dad still working at eleven o'clock on Christmas Eve? Did her parents have such a poor marriage that his hours didn't matter? Even without Levi, she'd make sure work didn't swallow her entire life. Even if she had no one to share it with.

She'd listen to one voicemail. Just one of the dozen.

"Heather, where are you? I love you. We need to—"

She tapped away from it, staring at her phone. Touched another.

"Heather, please tell me you're okay. There was a bad accident on I-90. I love you so much, I couldn't bear if anything happened to you."

A third.

"Please call me. I love you."

He was awfully busy phoning her for someone who had a celebrated actress drooling over him. She gave herself a mental slap. He'd never, ever indicated he wanted to get back with Tahira. He'd told Heather it was ancient history. That it wasn't his finest moment.

Heather's response hadn't been her finest, either. But that didn't mean she was ready to forget everything. On the other hand, this man was worried sick about her, and it wasn't fair to ignore that.

A text. She could do a text.

Hey, I'm at my parents' house in Missoula for a few days. Really need a break from everything. Don't worry.

She stared at the words for a minute. Tapped a bit more.

I'm sure you can't wait to get back to Seattle.

Send. And have a nice life. She stuffed the phone in her pocket and grabbed her carry-on. Nothing in the rest of her luggage or boxes would be damaged in the freezing temperatures overnight. It could all wait until morning. Because, when all was said and done, she wasn't so certain anymore that coming home had been the right thing to do.

Her phone rang again on her way up the walk.

OVER FORTY HOUSEHOLDS with the surname Francis were listed in Missoula. What was Heather's father's name? Levi had no idea. He sat in front of his laptop scrubbing his hands through his hair. How could he find her if she didn't want to be found?

"You still up, bro?" Jared appeared in the doorway in a black T-shirt and plaid pajama pants.

"Yeah. Sorry if I disturbed you."

"No. Not at all. My body's still trying to adjust to that fourteen-hour time difference. Came downstairs for a glass of water and saw your light on down here. It's past midnight. Santa won't come if you're awake, you know."

"Santa hasn't brought me anything for a good many years."

Jared dropped to the edge of Levi's bed across the room. "You're right. Every good and perfect gift comes from above."

"I'm starting to remember. It's also a bad idea to shove gifts back in a giver's face. Whether it's God's gift or someone else's." Levi met his brother's gaze for a long moment.

"Heather?"

He nodded. "She left partway through the banquet. She's at her parents' place, but she won't answer her phone."

Levi waved at his laptop. "Do you know how many Francises there are in Missoula?"

"You're going to phone her parents at this time of night?"

Levi let out a long breath and shook his head. "Worse. I'm going to drive down there and pound on their door."

"You're serious?"

"Never more so."

"Wow. Okay. But it's like a two hour drive. Dude, you can*not* show up there at three a.m.. You don't want to be that stalker guy."

He felt like that stalker guy trying to figure out which Francis was the right one. So far he'd eliminated a few whose addresses indicated apartments or trailer courts. Neither was likely from what he knew of her upbringing.

"What do you know about her dad? Not a first name, I take it."

"He's a financial advisor of some sort. Investor?" Levi turned back to his laptop and typed in a new search. "Charles Francis. Could that be him?"

Not that Jared knew anything Levi didn't.

His fingers flew over the keyboard again, back to the online white pages. Charles Francis. An address. Google maps. Street view. Whoa. That house was half the size of Grizzly Gulch Resort. Charles Francis had money.

Jared leaned over his shoulder. "That the place?"

"I think so." His brother was right. He couldn't show up like a madman at three in the morning. Seven wasn't too early, was it? What could he do for four hours? Because sleeping wasn't really an option.

Time to make brownies.

"HEATHER?" Mom nudged the living room drapery aside a little. "There appears to be a black sports car parked behind your car in the driveway."

"A... what?" Heather bundled her hair between her hands and tossed it over her shoulder. She needed a shower in the worst way. Sleeping on all that hair product never brought out her best look.

"A car." Mom peered out the window. "There's a cowboy hat in it." She said 'cowboy' like it was a curse.

"I... um..."

Her mother's perfectly plucked eyebrows rose. Even at six-thirty in the morning, she was completely put together.

Heather was not.

"Someone you know, perhaps?"

"Don't let him in."

Mom sniffed and let the drapery fall back. "It's not like anyone is pounding down the door."

Levi. He'd come. How had he found her? Should she wait for him to come in to meet her parents first thing? Or should she put her coat and boots on over her pajamas and go out there, trying to convince him to go away?

She didn't want him to go away. She wanted to believe the words she'd listened to over and over last night. "I love you," he'd said.

She wanted to tell him back. She wanted *him*.

The doorbell rang.

She was a mess. Hair every which way. No makeup. Hello Kitty pajamas. "No."

But Mom was already walking toward the door. Flinging it open like it was Door Number Three in a game show.

Gentle snowflakes drifted onto Levi's cowboy hat where he stood, dressed all in black like the first time she'd seen him, in the halo of the exterior light. His gaze flicked off her mother and straight into the depth of the room. He took a step forward. "Heather? I know it's early. It looked like someone was up. I saw the curtain move."

"Who do we have here?" Dad's voice, from behind her.

"Can we allow this man inside?"

Mom was seriously asking *her* if Levi was safe? Heather managed a nod. It was too late, anyway.

Levi closed the door behind himself and stood in the foyer with its marble pillars separating the space from the living room, holding a large package.

What was in that? Heather cleared her throat. Her parents' gazes swung to her. "Mom, Dad, this is Levi Esteban. Levi, my parents, Charles and Deidre."

Levi removed his hat and nodded.

"Pleased to meet you." Dad crossed the space and shook Levi's hand firmly. Then he glanced back at Heather. "At least, I think so."

Mom looked him up and down. "You're quite good-looking. How tall are you?"

Heather groaned. "Mom. Please don't. In fact, I'd really appreciate it if you and Dad could give us a few minutes."

Dad took Mom's arm. "We'll just be in the kitchen getting coffee started. Call if you need anything." He gave Heather a significant look and led her mother out of the room.

Leaving Heather staring at Levi with cotton balls in her

mouth. Her mom was right, though. He was sure good on the eyes. "What are you doing here?"

He set down his hat and package on the hall table. Toed off his cowboy boots. Held out both hands and took two steps toward her. "I love you, Heather. Can we start over?"

So ready yourself to pass through the gates, from old to new. Clear the way for Heather; make it clear, easy, and straight. Unfurl the banners that proclaim Heather is renewed!

She could pass through this gate. She held her hands toward him. He crossed the gap in four big strides and wrapped both arms around her, giving her a twirl that would have made a ballerina dizzy. Her arms wrapped around his neck, her hands buried in his thick, luscious hair. "Levi," she murmured. "I love you."

Their lips met, tasting, feeling, making her giddy. She'd missed him so much. His strong arms, the smoldering light in those green eyes.

But they still needed to be careful. Breathless, she pulled back a little, just as he did.

His eyes closed for a second then opened again, emotions pouring out of them that words couldn't express. "Heather. I can't believe this."

She wiggled until he set her down. "Me, either."

"Is there something we need to know?"

Trust Dad to be standing in the kitchen doorway watching. Not that she or Levi had done anything wrong. She slid an arm around Levi's waist and felt his wrap around her shoulder. "Did I forget to mention I have a boyfriend?"

Levi nuzzled her hair. "I like the sound of that. For now."

"It must be time to have a sit-down in my office then."

"Later, Dad." Much later. She looked up at Levi. "What's in the package?"

He grinned and kissed her cheek. "Breakfast."

"What?"

"Brownies for breakfast. All the biggest rage, I hear. I think mine have been voted the best west of the Mississippi. Want to give them a try?"

*Y*ou're really taking Opal's place?"

Levi could hardly believe it, either. "She wants to semi-retire and switch to part-time. Who knew she wanted to travel?"

Across the table from him, Heather rested her chin in her hand. "I'm surprised Dr. Mackie didn't ask Jared to be executive chef."

"They talked about it, but Jared says there's more to life than a promotion at work." He grinned at Heather. "Something I've come to understand, myself. Working day shift gives Jared more time with Aimee and the kids. Now that they're prepping for Yun's surgery, they're pretty focused on that."

"And Opal will cover Jared's shifts while they're away?"

He nodded, filling his eyes with her in the flickering candlelight. She was looking particularly stunning tonight.

They'd spent the past six weeks texting, phoning, and Skyping as Levi went back to work in Seattle, quickly deciding that cooking under Ellison Benoit wasn't for him.

Heather had gone to work with her dad. They'd shared their hopes, their dreams, and yes, their longings. He'd stopped in to see her last week in Missoula on his return trip to Helena. This time, to stay.

He'd invited her to Helena for the weekend and asked her to dress up for Valentine's dinner. No doubt she thought he'd take her to Lucca's but, after picking her up from Jase and Marisa's, he'd brought her to his own brand new apartment. He'd gone all out in a dinner for two, Mexican style. Didn't hurt to flaunt his roots occasionally.

"So... you think you might be open to moving back to Helena?" Levi managed to keep his face impassive.

"Well, I do love my new job." She gave him a flirtatious grin. "Numbers are so much more predictable than people."

This woman made him crazy. In a good way.

Heather tilted her head to one side. "On the other hand, I have been talking to Dr. Mackie. They could use a financial advisor, he said, and I could take on other clients in Helena. But Dad says I need six months of training before he'll turn me loose."

So, until the end of June? He could live with that. Just barely.

"That sounds reasonable." Levi's mouth went dry. It was time. "Ready for dessert?"

She patted her stomach. "I don't know if I could eat another bite."

Uh. Wrong answer. "You know you want to. I made something special."

"We could go for a walk first and make some room."

Still the wrong answer. "Sit tight." He moved into his tiny kitchen, plated two squares of brownies, and scooped

French vanilla bean ice cream to the side. Then the crowning touch, hard caramel he'd hand-drizzled into two-dimensional crowns. He'd made a dozen before one was just the right shape. Man, if he was going down, he was going all the way. One more little decoration, and he was ready.

"Close your eyes," he called from the kitchen.

"Okay."

He peered around the doorway. "You're peeking."

She scrunched her face. "Am not."

Levi set his own dessert down first then rounded the table and gently lowered hers. Turned it to just the right angle. Yes, the candlelight glinted just perfectly. "All right, you may look now."

He held his breath, watching her eyes catch the gleam of the candles. Watching them widen as she caught sight of the diamond ring circling the tip of the candy crown perched upright in the ice cream.

Levi dropped to one knee and slid his arm around the back of her chair. "Heather, will you marry me? I love you more than words can express."

She reached a trembling finger to touch the ring then drew back. "I don't know what to say."

"The only word I want to hear is 'yes'." She would, wouldn't she? But she was making him wait longer than he'd like.

Heather turned slightly in her chair. "Yes. Yes, Levi. I'll marry you."

She wrapped both arms around his neck as he scooped her up and gave her a twirl. Not as much room in this tiny apartment as in her parents' house, but that was okay. This was just a temporary landing spot. The important thing? She'd said "yes."

"When?" he murmured against her throat. "Please don't make me wait too long."

She kissed his nose as he set her back down, but stayed in the circle of his arms. "I'm kind of booked up until the end of June."

"So... the first weekend in July?"

"Sounds absolutely perfect. My mom's going to hate that it's less than eighteen months, but—"

"You're kidding me, right?"

Heather giggled. "Not at all. She's the one who loves all things festive, remember? She'll be hard done by to fit it all in in under five months."

Five months until he could claim his bride. But she was worth every minute of it.

DEAR READER...

Thanks for reading *Better Than a Crown*! I'm so honored that you chose to spend the last few hours with Heather, Levi, and me. You are appreciated.

I'm an independent author who relies on my readers to help spread the word about stories you enjoy. Would you take a few minutes to let your friends know on Facebook, Instagram... wherever you hang out online? Also, each honest review at online retailers means a lot to me and helps other readers know if this is a book they might enjoy. I'd sure appreciate your help getting word out.

I welcome contact from readers. At my website, you can contact me via email, read my blog, and find me on social media. You can also sign up for my newsletter to be notified of new releases, contests, special deals, and more! You'll receive *Promise of Peppermint*, the ebook novella that introduces my Urban Farm Fresh Romance series absolutely free as my thank you gift!

Keep reading for a sneak peek of another Christmas romance set in Montana, this time in a new series called

Saddle Springs Romance. I hope you enjoy this taste of *The Cowboy's Christmas Reunion*!

~ Valerie Comer
   www.valeriecomer.com
   http://valeriecomer.com/subscribe

Montana
Ranches
Christian Romance Series

THE
COWBOY'S
Christmas Reunion

SADDLE SPRINGS ROMANCE – BOOK 1

USA Today Bestselling Author
VALERIE COMER

THE COWBOY'S CHRISTMAS REUNION

CHAPTER 1

*S*o, how many households does that make?" Kade Delgado shifted his sleeping toddler in his arms, but Jericho snored on.

His buddy James Carmichael tapped a pen to his notebook. "Fifteen, including seven single moms with eighteen kids under the age of ten." He looked around the trio of cowboys. "Can we handle that many?"

"We can if Kade's brothers are in." Garret Morrison raised his eyebrows at Kade.

"Not sure if Sawyer is sticking around." The onset of winter might send his kid brother south, and the weatherman had called for an early storm. A glance out the window proved the forecast correct. A swirl of blowing snow peppered the glass, faintly illuminated by the lighted coffee shop sign.

Man, Kade should have come to Saddle Springs for groceries yesterday, but an injured heifer had kept him tied up. Or he should have denied his buddies' invitation to coffee while he was in town anyway. This could have been handled by email, couldn't it? He really needed to get going. The mountain road would be beyond sketchy and all the way to ugly soon — if it wasn't already.

"I'll have to double-check with both of them, but what's the alternative? Let some kid wake up with no gifts on Christmas morning?" Kade's arms tightened around his young son. "Let some old man or young mom struggle to shovel themselves out after a snowstorm — which, by the way, we're getting the mother of right now? Let's wrap this up."

Garret nodded. "Break them up geographically. I'll take the ones on the east side of town. That includes—" he leaned closer to James's notebook and circled part of the page with his finger "—Granny Talcott and the Yang family. Carmen Haviland. A couple more."

Geographically? Kade shook his head but didn't voice his thoughts. It only made sense, but that gave him the Mackenzies. They'd been reclusive even before their granddaughter, Cheri, had skipped town less than a week prior to her wedding to Kade and never looked back. Her choice sent her grandparents into a spin they hadn't recovered from in over six years. Neither had Kade. Not really.

He forced his mind back to the cozy coffee shop and nuzzled the top of Jericho's tousled head. It was past time to get all the way over Cheri. To man up and give her grandparents a good dose of Jesus' love. Mend some fences, literally and otherwise.

James angled a look at him. "That okay, Kade?"

"Sure." Maybe he could sic one of his brothers on Cheri's grandparents. "Look, I'll be back in town in a few days, but I really need to get Jer home and check the cattle before this storm blows in for real." He poked his chin toward James as he rose. "Send me an email."

The two-year-old struggled in his arms and rubbed sleep out of his eyes. "Daddy?"

"Yes, bucko?"

"I hungry."

The middle-aged barista bustled over carrying a plate of treats. "Here, little man. Let Auntie Abigail give you a cookie. Daddy won't mind."

Kade chuckled. "You're sneaky, Abigail." He slid Jericho to the floor and reached for his cowboy hat. Abigail's rules included hats off inside Java Springs. "Only one, bucko. We'll have supper when we get back to the ranch."

"Tanku," Jericho announced, helping himself to a cookie and giving Abigail a shy smile.

She held the plate toward Kade. "Have a couple for the road. I think I'll lock up behind you guys, even though it's a little early. I imagine everyone in Saddle Springs will haul in an extra armload of firewood and hunker down for the storm."

"I don't mind if I do." Kade plucked a pumpkin cookie studded with cranberries off the plate. "Thanks. These are great."

She turned toward the other guys as they shrugged into their jackets. Kade pulled out his key fob, started his truck with a press of the button, then knelt to tug Jericho's parka around the boy before zipping it.

Behind him, the coffee shop door swung open with a jingle of bells and a blast of Arctic air. He glanced over his shoulder and froze as solid as the Montana night.

Framed in the doorway stood Cheri Mackenzie. The

woman couldn't be anyone else. Her long blond hair, anchored with a dark knit hat, whipped in the snow-swirled wind, and a black wool coat covered her frame. Those blue eyes lassoed his like he was a faltering calf. The force of the shock was so great it took a second to realize a little girl who looked like her clung to her hand.

Didn't that just figure?

Kade rocked back on his heels and stood, pulling the brim of his cowboy hat down a smidgen. "Cheri. What a surprise."

James strode over and pulled the carved wooden door shut, but the newcomer didn't even seem to notice.

Maybe everyone else thought it was warmer in here without winter howling in, but it made no difference to Kade. The sight of her after all these years reminded him his heart had moved to the North Pole... and not to the cozy den housing Santa's workshop.

He hoisted Jericho into his arms and tore his gaze from hers long enough to nod to his friends. "See you."

"Can I pour you a coffee? Maybe get you some cookies?" Abigail bustled closer. "I was going to close up, but I can stay another half hour. Get you warmed up before you head back into this."

Cheri's eyes went from Kade's to Abigail's and back again. "My car is stuck."

Garret reached for his gloves. "Where about, ma'am? We can shovel you out. Get you on your way."

"It kind of slid off the highway when I turned into town." She bit her lip. "I'll need a tow truck, I think."

"Sully's gone down to Missoula early for Thanksgiving." Abigail glanced between the men with a worried frown.

"And Danny's got a broken leg. I don't know as there's someone else who can drive that rig."

"Can haul it out with the tractor if needed," said Garret.

James thumbed toward the darkened window "That's a job best done in daylight."

Everyone turned to Kade. Why, what did he have to do with this? Nothing. Nothing at all. Cheri had washed her hands of him and, after wallowing in disbelief and anger for a few weeks — okay, make that months — he'd washed his right back. He wasn't getting involved in anything within ten miles of Cheri Mackenzie ever again. In fact, he wouldn't even need to help out her grandparents for the Cowboy Santa project now that she was here. She could take care of them.

Except... didn't the mandate include single moms? But she probably wasn't single. Her husband had likely stayed by the car and sent her in to make a phone call.

Kade didn't have to lift a finger to help her. He swung Jericho to his left hip. "Sorry to hear of your troubles." Other than that they served her right. Being stuck in a snowbank was nothing compared to what she'd done to him.

"What brings you back to Saddle Springs?" Abigail asked.

Kade stared at Cheri, eyebrows raised. Wasn't that the question they all wanted the answer to? Other than Garret, who hadn't lived here back then.

Her gaze darted to his then back to Abigail. "Grandpa needs me. He fell and broke some ribs a few days ago and can't really manage the chores."

Cheri was a hundred pounds at most, wearing boots and

soaking wet. Didn't look like she'd put on any weight in the past six years. Unless she'd been doing some serious working out, she couldn't toss bales any more than Chester could. And weren't her grandparents down to two or three horses?

He sucked in his bottom lip. So much for the Mackenzies being off his list. Unless there really was a Mr. Cheri somewhere, but she kept saying *I* and *me*. Not *us* and *we*. Dead giveaway there.

"Your grandparents' spread is halfway up River Road, right?" put in James. "Kade is going right past on his way to Eaglecrest. He can probably drop you and your daughter off, and we can dig your car out tomorrow when the snow lets up."

"I couldn't ask."

Kade choked back a snort. She didn't have to, not with his buddies and Abigail being ever so helpful. His conscience bit hard. He'd forgiven her, hadn't he? If not, he'd at least moved on, in a manner of speaking. Married Daniela. Been widowed, which was only another way to leave a guy standing there in his sock feet with his hat off, trying to sort out what had happened. And through it all, God had quietly smoothed out rough places in his life and filled the dry creek beds.

He gave a curt nod. "We can do that. Like James says, I'm going right past anyway." Because half an hour ago, he'd signed on to fulfill God's mandate to help the widows and fatherless in their distress. Wasn't it like God to make him start with Cheri Mackenzie?

THE WARM GLOW from the windows of the coffee shop where she'd hung out so often as a teen had burned a welcoming beacon to Cheri as she struggled up the street, towing her daughter through snow that seemed to deepen even in the three blocks from the highway turnoff. It had seemed cozy and welcoming right until she'd stepped inside and seen Kade Delgado. Holding a toddler.

Then the Montana winter wind swirled around her heart once again. What had she been thinking, coming home? That she could keep on sneaking through town to the ranch as she'd done occasionally over the years? That she could hide out there for a month or two, helping her grandparents, with neither the nosy town of Saddle Springs nor the Delgados at Eaglecrest Ranch up the road any the wiser?

Now Abigail Evening crouched in front of her daughter, offering her a cookie. Harmony whispered a thank you as she accepted.

Cheri took a deep breath. "I'll get a room at the Hats Off Motel. If it's still in business." Not that she wanted to. Not when Grandpa and Grandma were expecting her tonight, but it had to be better than spending twenty minutes in the cab of Kade's truck.

All eyes stared at her.

"But, Mama..." Harmony looked up at her, tears catching on the ends of her eyelashes.

"I can drive you." Kade's words were polite enough, but there was only steel in those brown eyes. "Chester can bring you down to get your car in a day or two. We'll leave a note for Sully and the State Patrol so they know it's not abandoned." He poked his chin toward the door. "Truck's already running just outside. Ready?"

She'd never be prepared, but she nodded anyway. "Thanks."

"That's settled, then." Abigail beamed like she'd directed the Helena Symphony. Maybe she thought she had.

Kade pushed the door open and held it, forcing Cheri to brush past him. Even with the snow battering her face, the scent she smelled was all Kade. Horses. Leather. And a hint of woodsy aftershave. Memories flooded her, memories she shoved aside. He had a kid. He was married. Off limits... not that she was exactly free herself.

The other two cowboys came out behind them, slapping backs and promising to keep in touch. And here she'd thought it was women who had hen parties.

Kade opened the passenger door of the big black Chevy idling at the curb then the door behind it. "Hop in," he said to Harmony, still holding his little guy. Always the gentleman. He shut the doors behind them both then rounded the truck and tucked his boy into the car seat. A minute later he was in the driver's seat. "Need anything from your car? Suitcase? Booster, maybe?"

"That would be helpful. Thank you."

A few minutes later, her bags in the truck bed, Kade flipped on the four-wheel drive and pointed the truck west across the bridge and up the mountain road. Swirling snow blocked visibility, but Cheri relaxed. At least she didn't have to drive in this mess anymore. She could trust Kade.

"So... your daughter." Kade flicked a glance into the rearview mirror.

Some wouldn't believe she wasn't Kade's child, but he

knew. She knew. "Her name is Harmony. She'll be six in April." Let him do the math.

He shot her a tight glance barely discernible in the glow of the truck's instrument panel. "Who's her father?"

Yep, he'd done the math. Harmony had been born nine months after the wedding that hadn't happened. Cheri shook her head. She wasn't ready to go there with Kade. Dredge open the whole mess from that horrible summer. "Your son looks a lot like you."

His lips tightened. "His name is Jericho."

Jericho. Kade had always liked that name. Planned to name his first son that since he'd been a teen. Memories of long kisses in the apple orchard amid glorious fragrant blossoms blocked out the blowing snow for just a moment. They'd shared their hopes and promises and dreams. Until she'd ruined everything.

She blinked the dark night back into focus. Flakes stabbed at the windshield as the four-by-four rounded one more curve in the climb out of Saddle Springs. "Congratulations," she whispered. "I hope you're very happy."

The truck slid a little and Kade's gloved hands tightened on the wheel. Was the grim set of his chin because of the road conditions, the shock of seeing her again... or because his life wasn't full of joy?

The gates of Paradise Creek Ranch ghosted from the darkness, and Kade turned his truck to crawl down the long drive. Cheri couldn't help the worry that he wouldn't make it back out again, but he was a good driver, and the truck seemed nearly new. She dared to breathe again when the lights of the old ranch house came into view.

"Here you go." Kade lifted the bags out of the back, set

them on the porch, and brushed a couple of inches of snow off them.

"Thanks." She helped Harmony down as the door opened and Grandma peered out.

"Thank goodness you made it!"

Cheri wrapped her grandmother in a hug. "More like thank Kade. My car is stuck in town, but we can get it in a day or two."

Grandma's eyebrows shot up. "Kade Delgado?"

"Ma'am." He tipped his hat as he turned away. "I'll be on my way home now."

She flinched as though he'd struck her. "You can't."

Kade swung back toward Grandma. "Pardon me?"

"Chester is listening to the scanner. There's an avalanche across the road at mile eighteen, by the hairpin curve. Won't be anyone getting through tonight. Took down all the lines, too."

He opened his mouth, snapped it shut again, and stared at Cheri, his gaze burning into hers for a long moment. "It's too far back to town."

It had taken them nearly an hour to crawl the twenty-minute trip. There'd been a lot of silence that matched the weather, past chilly and on to deep freeze. And now Grandma was suggesting *what* exactly?

Kade's gaze swung to Grandma. "May I borrow Chester's snowmobile?"

"It's broke down. He ordered parts last week. You and your boy will need to stay the night, I guess."

Cheri winced at the graceless words, but Grandma was right. If the road up to Eaglecrest was blocked, he didn't have any choice. "Harmony can sleep with me tonight. That will leave the other bedroom for Kade and Jericho. Maybe it will all look better in daylight." She could only hope.

From the truck came the bellow of an unhappy toddler. Still Kade stood, looking from one to the other. Then he pulled a cell phone out of his pocket, glanced at it, rolled his eyes, and shoved it back in. There'd never been decent coverage deep in this valley.

"I'd be obliged, ma'am. Thank you."

Wait. What? Just like that she'd be spending another twelve hours or more in the same house as Kade Delgado?

No, please, Lord. Hadn't she been punished enough?

The Cowboy's Christmas Reunion
is available in paperback
wherever you purchased
Better Than a Crown!

ABOUT VALERIE COMER

Valerie Comer's life on a small farm in western Canada provides the seed for stories of contemporary Christian romance. Like many of her characters, Valerie grows much of her own food and is active in the local foods movement as well as her church. She only hopes her imaginary friends enjoy their happily-ever-afters as much as she does hers, shared with her husband, adult kids, and adorable granddaughters.

Valerie is a *USA Today* bestselling author and a two-time Word Award winner. She writes engaging characters, strong communities, and deep faith into her green clean romances.

To find out more, visit her website at www.valeriecomer.com, where you can read her blog, explore her many links, and sign up for her monthly email newsletter, where you will find news, giveaways, deals, book recommendations and more. You can also find Valerie blogging with other authors of Christian contemporary romance at Inspy Romance.